Principal Bagwell, Say It Ain't So!

Joseph Rodney

CENTAUR BOOKS
·CHICAGO·

• Chicago •

Principal Bagwell, Say It Ain't So!

Joseph Rodney

Published by
Centaur Books
• Chicago •
CentaurBooks.com

13-Digit ISBN: 978-1-941049-25-9

Disclaimer:
This is a work of fiction. Names, characters, places, and incidents are the product of the author's imagination or have been used fictitiously. Any resemblance to actual persons, living or dead, events, locales or organizations is entirely coincidental.

Printed in the United States of America

Dedication

To my father and mother,
who have always been there for me
on this roller coaster we call life. If
there are two better people than my
parents out there in the world,
I would like to meet them.

Table of Contents

Part I

Chapter 1

Living the Dream

Tuesday, October 10

Tapping my pencil on my desk and humming along to the tune of "Eye of the Tiger," I realize this is one of the better days I have had in quite a while. No meetings! No out-of-control students! No phone calls from irate parents! What more can a principal ask for on a Tuesday?

It is now 3:45 PM, and I've made it through another uneventful day. Oh, I almost forgot to introduce myself. My name is Nyles Bagwell, and I am the principal of a prestigious K–8 public school named Westmoreland Learning Academy, located in Myrtle Beach, South Carolina. The school has 630 students currently enrolled, and I have been the principal for the past nineteen years.

My friends not in education say I am the luckiest guy alive because I get the summers off and many random breaks. I chuckle when they say this, knowing full well they don't know what they are talking about. With the daily stress, I tend to internalize even though I say I don't. I say I am living the dream when asked about my day. I mean it every time I say it. Who wouldn't? My two kids are part of the 630 students attending Westmoreland. My wife teaches a third-grade class at Westmoreland as well. Lucky, no! I feel blessed to have my whole family together because I know eventually this won't be the case. "Enjoy it now," I keep telling myself. And I do!

My wife, Jenny, has been here with me at Westmoreland for the past nineteen years. She is one of those people who always have a smile on the face. How sickening, right? If she isn't the best teacher in the district, she has to be one of the top three, in my opinion. I may be a little biased. She makes teaching look SO easy. She does have one fault; she is a worrywart. She would earn a gold medal for this life skill. You know those types of people who have to be at the airport three hours before the plane departs? Yes, that is her! It drives me crazy, but she gave me two phenomenal kids. I think I was put on this planet to be a father. I truly do!

My quiet, athletic, no-nonsense twelve-year-old son, MJ, brings so much joy into my life. His birth was truly one of the best days of my life. His sweet nature and dark, deep blue eyes made him on that day (and it is still true to this day) perfect. He is currently in seventh grade and wants to play in the MLB when he gets older. Or is it the NBA? He changes his mind every year, and it is hard to keep up. Last month, he told me he wants to go to Syracuse University. Just yesterday, he said he wants to move to San Diego after high school. What? That is what I love about him. He says things that are unpredictable and is open to possibilities.

Where do I even start about my nine-year-old daughter, Chloe? She LOVES school. No, I really mean she LOVES school. Maybe it is because her mom and I are both educators here at Westmoreland. Maybe it is because of the great teachers she has had. She has a problem, though. She is crazy about reading. She reads more than anybody I have ever met, and she is only nine. I am making a prediction right here and now. She is going to be a teacher later on in life. I'm thinking, a kindergarten teacher. No, let's say third grade like her mom. Her spirit and passion toward school and life inspire me daily.

Once again, I will say it out loud. I am living the dream, day in and day out. What could go wrong? Well . . .

Chapter 2

My Secret #1

Friday, October 20

Have you ever had one of those days when you wake up and everything goes wrong from the time you step out of bed? No worries, me too! I am not talking about spilling orange juice on your shirt or getting a D+ on your math quiz even though you studied. Think bigger! How about when you accidentally leave part of your breakfast in your beard? That happened to me once walking into a fifth-grade classroom. I remember it like yesterday. I was observing Ms. Albright's classroom, usually for five to ten minutes every Thursday or Friday. While the students were quietly working on their geography worksheet about the Great Lakes, a few of the students kept guffawing and giggling about something. I couldn't put my thumb on it until a student named Drew Daze finally had the courage to tell me.

"Mr. Bagwell, can you kneel down by my desk?" he whispered.

"Sure, Drew. How can I help you?" I inquired.

You can figure out the rest of the conversation by yourself. Gross! I ran out of the room faster than a bolt of lightning. I did see Drew in the hallway a few times later that week. He would always give me a thumbs-up. How embarrassing!

Having food on your face is really not that big of a deal. I'm still talking about a day that you wish you could hit the Rewind button and start all over again. Or feel sorry for yourself and say, "Why me?"

Where do I start? I have a secret I am mortified to tell anyone, but I'm afraid that somebody is going to find out. Not even my wife knows. And I tell her everything! But as you remember, my wife has one shortcoming. She is a worrywart, and I'm afraid to tell her because I know she will get very stressed out about it. She will get violently sick, throwing up in the toilet, and then she will ask a million questions that I don't want to answer. Yes, one million questions! So why tempt fate? Not happening!

It all started when I went to a principals' conference in Atlantic City, New Jersey. I have to admit I didn't have a positive outlook going to these conferences. Leaving my wife alone with the kids seemed like a punishment to her while I was enjoying myself on almost something like a mini-vacation even though I was working. Well, kind of! LOL. When I get home from these conferences that range anywhere from being gone from one to five days, I usually get a death glare from my wife. I don't think she is mad at me, but she is tired from watching the kids by herself. She usually plans a GNO (girls' night out) with her girlfriends for the next weekend. I can't complain. She deserves it.

Well, anyway, back to my secret about how it all started! I've been sitting here with tears in my eyes about how to tell you. It is extremely hard to share a secret with anybody, especially one of this magnitude. If you don't mind, I'm not ready to share this with you yet. I will eventually! Just give me a little more time, and I will open up about it. My apologies! If I were you and somebody told me they were going to share a big secret about themselves and then didn't tell me, I would be annoyed. Sorry! You will see, as you read more about me, I say sorry a lot. I picked this habit up from my wife. Until tomorrow!

Chapter 3

October Break

Saturday, October 21

I must have rolled over from one shoulder to the next every thirty minutes last night in bed. Have you ever done that before? I tend to do this once a week, maybe more especially lately. My brain is working like sixty. I guess I'm not ready to tell others my secret quite yet. So . . .

Let's switch to something more positive and entertaining to talk about. My wife and I decided a few weeks ago to surprise the kids and go on a mini-vacation during our October break, which starts today. As I am writing this at 5:02 AM, we will be waking up the kids in three hours and packing the car for sunny Orlando, Florida. I can hear you laughing while you are reading. Why in the world would you go to Florida since we live in Myrtle Beach? Head toward the mountains and spend the week in a cabin or go sightseeing and see something historic, like the Statue of Liberty or Mount Rushmore. I hear ya, but I was vetoed by the boss, my wife. Since we have never taken the kids to Disney World, I gave in pretty easily. The kids have begged us for three years now. They will be awestruck when we get there and see the Tower of Terror, which I am looking forward to immensely. It is seven to eight hours' drive to Disney, so I am going to stop writing for now. I will do my best to write sometime next week.

Chapter 4

Are You Kidding Me?

Thursday, October 26

I promised myself I wouldn't write about how great of a time we are having, but man, I could come here every year and be happy. Coming to Disney in October is not too shabby. Friends of ours said it wouldn't be as crowded in October. It isn't 100 degrees with rainy thunderstorms like what you think of when you think of Orlando. They were right! So I'm not going to brag about all of the sensational things we have done. I would like to share a couple of stories with you about our family vacation you might find amusing.

My nine-year-old, Chloe, is always on her phone. I know, I know. She is nine and has a phone already. Don't judge me! She is spoiled, and I always give in when she wants something. The first, second, and third time she asks for something, I say no, but I love to see her on cloud nine. She deserves it! She works hard at school, and she should be rewarded for her effort.

Anyway, driving down to Disney, Chloe was looking up jokes on her phone to share with me. My wife falls asleep in the first thirty minutes of every trip. My son, MJ, puts on his headphones and listens to music until we stop at the gas stations or rest areas.

So Chloe decided to keep me awake and alert. She was going to tell me jokes. I told her that it was 11:00 AM, and I was wide awake . . . no worries!

She still insists on sharing the hysterical jokes which crack her up. She always says, "Dad, this one is better than the last one." I don't have the heart to tell her I have heard all of these jokes. Heck, it makes the drive more bearable.

All of a sudden, she told me the best joke that I had never heard before. I laughed so hard it woke up Jenny. I was laughing so much I accidentally farted. I have no idea how that happened! Obviously, that made Chloe laugh uncontrollably, which started the whole family breaking up for a good five minutes. The figure of speech for this outburst would be categorized as somebody who would be "rolling in the aisles" or "be doubled up in stitches." I have to share this joke with you so you can pass it on to somebody who has a good sense of humor.

Chloe paused and whispered, "Dad, here is a good one!"

"Go ahead, sweetheart," I responded.

"How do you make holy water?" she asked.

I thought for a moment. I couldn't come up with a funny reply, so I just said, "I'm not sure."

She excitedly cried out, "You boil the H*** out of it!"

You might have heard that joke before, but I never have. Next, I know what you are thinking. My nine-year-old just said a bad word. I did talk to her about it and told her it might not be appropriate for some audiences. Kids love to laugh and joke around. Chloe is definitely one of those kids.

MJ, on the other hand, is my quiet child. Remember, it is hard for him to get a word in sometimes sitting by Chloe, who enjoys talks. He came up with a great idea that we should go to Gatorland instead of a Disney park one day. Well, I actually thought it was a great idea. I have always wanted to go there since way back when I was a kid. So I thought, why not? Sounds like fun! You know where this is going, right? What could go wrong?

I know you think that I got bitten by an alligator and maybe lost a finger, right? Good try, but your prediction would be incorrect. When we were watching a show that the professional alligator handlers were conducting, I was "fortunate" enough to be picked as a volunteer even though I wasn't raising my hand. Why me? I strolled up toward the handlers with my family cheering me on as I got closer and closer to my death. Let me be clear about something. My family knows I am only afraid of two things, Ferris wheels and snakes. I am not afraid of alligators. I actually enjoy them when I know the gator will have black duct tape around its mouth. I have seen this on television before. Some unsuspecting fool is picked and has to hold a small alligator with both of his or her hands. Big deal, huh? That is what I thought too.

What was the next reptile that came out from behind me while I was holding the baby alligator? Yes, snakes! One of the handlers put the snake (let's call him Satan) around my neck. I nervously panicked, and I think I said a bad word. Not one of my better moments. I heard MJ scream, "Dad, watch out! The snake might bite you!" Many things ran through my head at this time. I wanted to throw the snake 50 yards like a Cam Newton touchdown pass to his wide receiver. I just froze like a deer in the headlights. Thirty seconds later (or what felt like thirty minutes later), the same handler took the snake off me. Why? Because I was scared? Nope! The slimy, slithery snake decided to be a wise guy and peed on me. Why me?

We are here in beautiful Orlando, Florida, for one more day. Then, back to reality until our next break, which is Thanksgiving. It is only four weeks away, so I can't complain too much. I'm not sure when I will be able to write again. The workdays after a vacation when I come back are crazy chaotic. I tend to go to bed early. This means I don't have the energy to write late at night or early before I start the school day. My wife and kids don't even know I have a journal that I write in every once in a while. Jenny thinks I am doing paperwork for school.

One of my favorite things to do is to share a positive motivational quote with my students every morning at school. I do this via the intercom when school starts at 8:00 AM. The next time I write in my journal, I am going to share some of my favorite quotes with you. These messages make me feel good inside. I hope they do the same for you.

Chapter 5

One Can Dream

Sunday, November 12

Everybody has their favorites: foods, movies, colors, sports, etc. I have those as well, but I also have a favorite quote. I am in the career of education, so I have not just one favorite quote but many. Here are the top ten quotes I enjoy.

1. "No one is perfect. That's why pencils have erasers." (Author unknown)
2. "You're off to great places! Today is your day! Your mountain is waiting, so get on your way!" (Dr. Seuss)
3. "Nothing is impossible. The word itself says 'I'm possible.'" (Audrey Hepburn)
4. "Choose a job you love, and you will never have to work a day in your life." (Confucius)
5. "Never waste a minute thinking of anyone you don't like." (Eisenhower)
6. "No act of kindness, no matter how small, is ever wasted." (Aesop)
7. "Be a rainbow in someone else's cloud." (Maya Angelou)
8. "If you can dream it, you can do it." (Walt Disney)
9. "Shoot for the moon. Even if you miss, you'll land among the stars." (Les Brown)
10. "If you see someone without a smile, give them one of yours." (Dolly Parton)

If I had to pick one of these quotes that is my favorite, I would probably say, "Choose a job you love, and you will never have to work a day in your life." I know many friends who complain about how much they dislike their job, and they wish they could quit. Whether it was because of their lack of pay, long hours, boss, or something else, each one of them seems unhappy. Don't get me wrong. I have many days I wish I worked as a taxi driver or in retail at Macy's department store, not as a principal. I can always say each week I have one amazing day, three average days, and one day that I try to hide in my office and not come out. But I wouldn't trade my job for anything in the whole world. Well, maybe free pizza every day of the year and a money tree in the backyard.

Does anyone have one of those Aladdin lamps you can rub and a genie comes out to grant you three wishes? What would your wishes be? You know two of mine: free pizza and a money tree. My last wish undoubtedly would have to be for MJ and Chloe to be happy and successful throughout their whole life. I love my kids so much, and I can't wait to see what lies ahead for them in five, ten, and fifteen-plus years down the road. I love to ponder about what could or might happen.

My hope is that you enjoyed these positive quotes, and my goal is to share some more with you later on in my journal. Time for bed. I'm going to be exhausted tomorrow. Monday morning blues!

Chapter 6

Indiana, Here We Come!

Sunday, November 19

A week has passed since I last wrote in my journal. I'm thinking I want to start off each journal entry from now on with a positive quote. If you don't think that would be a good idea, too bad! I'm going to do it anyway. Ha!

How about, "Don't bunt. Aim out of the ballpark!" I love this quote written by David Ogilvy, who is known by old-timers as the father of advertising. There is your fact of the day. My mom and dad always used to tell me if I wanted to be smart, I should learn one new fact every day. You know what? I didn't believe them then, but I do now.

I did make a decision earlier this week. My plan was to write my secret in this journal over Christmas break. Originally, I thought maybe over Thanksgiving break, but I changed my mind as the week progressed. Why? No reason, really, I just did. If you can bear with me, you have my promise that I will tell you my secret next month. Stay tuned!

This week, we only have school on Monday and Tuesday because of the Thanksgiving holiday on Thursday. My family travels to Indianapolis, Indiana, to visit my wife's side of the family for Thanksgiving. We will leave on Wednesday morning, and it takes approximately twelve long, excruciating hours to get there. Good old Indiana! The vast land of cornfields and chilly temperatures this time of the year. Myrtle Beach beats Indianapolis all day long. I really despise the cold. HATE it! But, my kids always have fun seeing and horsing around with their cousins. Of course, Jenny enjoys spending time with her family too. Me? Fake smiles for three and a half days until my jaw hurts. It wouldn't be so bad, but just like in every family, there is always that "one" relative. On my wife's side of the family, his name is Earl. He is my wife's brother who constantly talks about the most moronic happenings currently going on in the world. His wife, Anna, and their two kids, Chris and Leesa (twins—one boy and one girl), are the sweetest people in the world. For the life of me, I don't have the foggiest idea of how Anna can stand to listen to Earl all day, every day.

For example, last year, Earl told me this story that a guy was planning on robbing a bank, so he paid a wizard (yes, a wizard) $500 to make him invisible. This made him believe that no one could see him, so he went into the bank and started snatching money right out of people's hands. I went back and forth with him, which was stupid to do because he thinks he is never wrong about his stories being malarkey and nonsense. You know what? I looked the story up on my phone, and sure enough, he was right! I hate it when I'm wrong, especially when I'm around Earl. You get the idea, though. That story took about thirty minutes to tell since he likes to add a whole bunch of funny quips, as he calls them, into the story. It might be okay if that was the only story, but he had many, many more. No worries, I will share another story of his from this year's get-together eventually. If I have to suffer, you will as well. As I sat there and listened to him ramble on and on, all I can say is, "Why me?"

Chapter 7

Here, Kitty, Kitty!

Thursday, November 23

Since today is Thanksgiving, how about a quote of the day? Be thankful for each new challenge because it will build your strength and character. I'm not sure who to give credit for regarding this quote, but I love reading it over and over. I guess I'm thankful for being able to spend time with my extended family, and I really enjoy seeing my kids laugh, frolic, and play with their cousins whom they don't get to see a lot.

I'm sitting at the kitchen table writing tonight. Everybody else is asleep in a food coma from all of the delicious delicacies that we devoured all day long. Seriously, why do I eat this much every Thanksgiving? My wife then wakes me up super early to go Black Friday shopping, which I dislike immensely. It rates right up there with picking up dog poop in my backyard. I guess I should be more thankful. I need to reread my quote above. Black Friday shopping is a challenge. If I look at it positively, it does build strength and character. Not patience, though! I would prefer to write about Earl and his cockamamie stories instead, though, so . . .

Here's a funny story about my brother-in-law, Earl, and his antics from earlier today. While a slew of us adults were sitting around, talking about our jobs, politics, the miserable weather, and other uninteresting topics, Earl chimed in out of nowhere about a tornado that touched down in their town a couple of months ago. My first reaction was he was lying because I would have heard about it already from my wife. So I whispered to Jenny, "Is he making this up?" She quietly mumbled, "No, I forgot to tell you about the tornado story." I thought to myself, how in the world can you forget to tell me about a tornado that almost took my in-law's life, for goodness' sake!

He was telling the story about this F4 tornado, which I later found out was an F2, laughing about how much damage occurred. I was bewildered by his laughing the whole time while he was telling his version of the story, and then I found out. He bragged that in the two minutes the twister had come and gone, the tornado had picked up several items and deposited them into his fenced backyard. He was now the proud owner of a swing set, trampoline, two bikes, and a talking cat that can say yes or no. I couldn't take it anymore! I, along with everybody else in the room, started to laugh hysterically. I literally had tears coming out of my eyes. After several minutes of uncontrollable hysterics, I finally decided to call his bluff. He had some crazy stories before, but this one was too over the top to believe. Until he showed me a video of his cat he had named Cyclone actually muttering those words when he was getting his fur brushed. Once again, he was right, and I was wrong. I didn't dare have the nerve to ask him if he had kept all of those items since they did not belong to him. I guess I didn't want to listen to his long-winded explanation. A talking cat!

I need to go to bed because I am getting up EARLY to go shopping. Yippee! Why me? I actually think the next time I write, I am going to share with you my secret. It is always on my mind, and I can't stop thinking about it. I need to tell somebody before I burst! Happy Thanksgiving, and bring on Christmas. Gobble, gobble!

Chapter 8

My Secret #2

Sunday, December 9

// If you have an important point to make, don't try to be subtle or clever. Use a pile driver. Hit the point once. Then, come back and hit it again. Then, hit it a third time with a tremendous whack." This is a quote that you need to read a couple of times and try to let it sink in. Go ahead, I'll wait. You better have read it at least one more time. Please read it one more time before you keep reading the rest of this chapter. The quote above is from Winston Churchill, an influential prime minister of the United Kingdom from 1940 to 1945 and again from 1951 to 1955. He has so many amazing quotes that I highly recommend you looking him up on the internet or reading a book about him. One fact I know about him is he did not do well in school as a child. If you are struggling as well, keep working hard like he did, and you too might be successful later in life.

You have waited long enough! I have actually cried so many times thinking about what I did. I am embarrassed, humiliated, and distressed about it times a million. Please don't think of me as a corrupt person. I am far from it. I made a bad mistake, and I don't know how to solve it even though I have a master's degree from a prestigious university. I guess they didn't teach me what to do when you make a really idiotic decision that could ruin your career. Like I said before, I was at a principals' conference in Atlantic City, New Jersey. I went to the casino to gamble each night just for something to do with a couple of other principals that were going and invited me. It sounded like fun. Since I am a pretty normal, boring guy, I thought this is something I would not do back home. I actually did above average for not really knowing what I was doing. I tried the slot machines and lost fifty dollars in just under thirty minutes. What a waste of money! I think I pulled that stupid arm down over a hundred times and only won once or twice. I moved onto blackjack, and I did much better. At least on the first night. The next four nights, I lost over $5,000 playing this addicting game. I kept telling myself that the odds were in my favor to start getting some of my money back. Unfortunately, Lady Luck was not on my side.

Knowing full well I didn't want to tell my wife that I lost $5,000 gambling, I did what every other man would do. I sat in my hotel room and panicked. Plan B would have to be in motion. What was Plan B? Well, my logical brain told me that I could win the money back by placing a bet or two on some National Football League (NFL) games that were going to be played on Sunday, which was two days away. I needed to pick a couple of upsets, so I could win my money back faster. Picking an upset would win me more money because I would be picking the team that was supposed to lose. After doing some research on the internet and watching ESPN talk about the teams, I decided to pick the Bears to beat the Packers and the Dolphins to beat the Patriots.

You can imagine what happened next. I was now home from the conference, intently watching both games. The Bears vs. Packers came on the television at 1:00 PM, while the Dolphins vs. Patriots didn't start until 8:30 PM. Jenny even asked me why I was watching football since normally I don't, but she didn't seem suspicious of anything, thankfully. As the Bears vs. Packers game was finishing up three hours after it started, I felt like throwing up. The Bears lost 38–13 in a blowout. Good pick, huh? I only lost another $1,000 on this game. In the second game, I could win $7,500 if the Dolphins beat the mighty Patriots. Eating dinner that night wasn't going to happen. I told Jenny I was still full from eating at the all-you-can-eat buffet in Atlantic City all week. At half-time, the score was tied 17–17, so I wasn't too worried quite yet about the outcome. Jenny, MJ, and Chloe stopped in from time to time to talk, get some help on homework, and say good night. I felt bad since I seemed to ignore all three of them all day, but you don't think straight when your mind is elsewhere. Jenny seemed annoyed when she poked her head in the room and exclaimed, "I put the kids to bed. No worries!" Ouch! All I could say was sorry. She stomped off in haste, but who could blame her since I barely have spoken to her all day. I can make it up to her tomorrow.

As the 11:00 PM hour rolls around, the Dolphins are actually beating the Patriots 30–17 beginning the fourth quarter. I actually start to relax a little for the first time all day. As the time kept ticking away, sure enough, the Patriots were creeping closer. They scored a touchdown to make the score 30–24 with six minutes left to play. On the next series of plays for the Dolphins, they marched the ball down the field to ultimately miss a field goal that would have put the Dolphins ahead by nine points with just a little over two minutes left in the game. C'mon, defense! Please come up big and force a turnover. Long story, short. Tom Brady, the Patriots quarterback, threw a touchdown to one of his favorite targets, Julian Edelman, for the winning score. I know for a fact from reading the sports section and watching Sports Center, a lot of football fans dislike Tom Brady. You know what? I am now not a fan either. The Patriots won 31–30. Now, I am not $5,000 in debt; I am $10,000 in debt.

I haven't even got to my secret yet. You might be thinking my secret was I didn't tell my wife about the money I had lost, but that is NOT the secret. I had to come up with another plan (let's call it Plan C) to somehow, someway get $10,000 before my wife noticed our missing funds. Stupid Bears! Stupid Dolphins! Stupid me! Why . . . Why . . . Why me? By the way, you might be thinking Jenny will notice the money missing from the bank account. Well, you hopefully would be wrong. All of these years we have been married, I have done all of the banking and paid the bills. She doesn't even use the checkbook. She uses her credit and debit card all of the time. God bless her for being naive about our bank account. She did mention last month that she was thinking about downloading the banking app on her phone. She hasn't mentioned it again, so I am pretty sure she forgot. Or did she?

Chapter 9

It Only Gets Worse

Sunday, December 16

Quote of the day: "A prudent person foresees danger and takes precautions. The simpleton goes blindly on and suffers the consequences." My wife's friend, Sara, this morning at church shared this from the book of Proverbs in the Bible. Unfortunately, I believe she was talking directly to me! Thankfully, she does not know of my predicament. Maybe I should talk to her for some advice? No chance! When students are struggling, I tell students, "Let's see if the counselor is available or talk to your friend." Why am I not taking my own advice? Embarrassment? Stubbornness? Ignorance? Yep! Yep! Yep!

SO HERE IT IS! My secret! Let me take a deep breath before I write it down. Argh! If I get caught, there is going to be a brouhaha for sure. My plan C was to "borrow" $10,000 from a rainy day account from my school. That way, I could quickly deposit the $10,000 into my bank account without my wife ever finding out. The only problem I could see with this plan was how I would get the $10,000 to put back into the school account without somebody finding out. I decided I would worry about this problem later.

The person who goes over the school accounts does not do anything until the end of the school year in June, which means I have plenty of time to figure this out. I am not a big fan of the school accountant and never have been. Not sure why. Maybe it is her name, Riley Reilly. That is not a typo. She doesn't smile much, and it is hard to have a conversation with her. When she stops by my office, I pretend I am working on something very important. Luckily, I don't have to worry about her for many months yet.

The good news is, this upcoming week, we only have three days of school because of winter break. My kids, MJ and Chloe, are super excited about the short week, and I 100 percent agree with them! I have been so worried and preoccupied lately. It will be nice to have two weeks off to spend quality time with Jenny, MJ, and Chloe.

I am not planning on writing in my journal for a while. If you don't hear from me, please have a merry Christmas and a happy New Year! It looks like I received an early Christmas gift. Ten thousand dollars. Why do I feel so rotten then?

Chapter 10

It Might Be, It Could Be, It Is!

Wednesday, January 3

Quote of the day: This is from Mark Twain, who was a famous American writer. His real name was Samuel Langhorne Clemens. Two of his most famous novels were *The Adventures of Tom Sawyer* and *The Adventures of Huckleberry Finn*. He had many quotes, but this is one of his best, in my opinion. "Twenty years from now, you will be more disappointed by the things that you didn't do than by the ones you did do, so throw off the bowlines, sail away from safe harbor, and catch the trade winds in your sails. Explore, dream, discover." Love this quote!

This holiday season was somewhat different than previous ones as of late. Let's say since MJ and Chloe were born. Normally, smiles and laughter overtake our house like no other in the last week of December and the first week of January. I'm not saying it didn't, but it seemed forced! How do you describe that your emotional state is scattered? Maybe fake? My mind seems to be elsewhere. Shocker!

I went into school yesterday for a few hours to finish up some reports that are due in a couple of days after we get back from the holiday break, which will be in five more days. I daydreamed a lot and wasn't myself. I felt like my job eventually could be in danger if I didn't get a handle on my problems. I felt like frozen orange juice. I could get canned, and I couldn't concentrate. In the last ten minutes, I sat at my desk and sobbed, teary-eyed from the stress and worry that I had brought on myself from my secret. Why me?

Once I arrived at home, I sat in the driveway for a few minutes, not able to move. If I don't get over this funk here quickly, I am going to go crazy! The song "What a Wonderful World" by Louis Armstrong came on the radio, which helped to pick up my spirits. It is like God knew I was struggling and sent that calming song to help me. If I only knew what was going to happen two minutes later, I would have stayed in the car.

Jenny was relaxing on the couch, watching a rerun of *The Housewives* . . . of some city. She had tears running down her cheeks, so I sarcastically mumbled, "What happened? Did somebody on the show die?" She gave me a blank stare and said, "No, but we need to talk." My throat tightened, and my stomach got a huge knot in it. She knew about my problem, but how could she? I felt like running out of the house and not stopping until I got to Lake Michigan, where I would bury myself in the sand so nobody could find me. Feeling like I wanted to sing the song "Babe" by Styx to Jenny as I strolled out the door came to my mind. I was frozen and just stood there like a deer in headlights.

She composed herself and quietly said three words to me, "I am pregnant." It might be, it could be, it is! Grand-slam game-winning home run! To say I was surprised would be an understatement! Can I write any more exclamatory sentences in this paragraph? Yes, I can. Oh my gosh! What is happening? At our age, we will be changing diapers AGAIN! After we hugged for several minutes and shed happy tears, I exclaimed, "Well!" That was all that came out of my mouth, and we didn't talk about baby number 3 until later that night when we lay down in bed. One thing for sure, it took my mind off my problem, which was a good thing. Maybe we can have a baby shower, and our friends and family can give us cash instead of baby clothes, bottles, pacifiers, or diapers. Wishful thinking! I am forty-nine years old, Jenny is forty-four, so we will call baby number 3 a miracle. Grandpa? No! Dad . . . Yikes!

Chapter 11

Fire in the Hole

Friday, January 12

Quote of the day: My daughter, Chloe, always says this, so I am stealing it from her. She got it from my angelic mother, and Chloe has never forgotten it. "Turn your attitude into gratitude." This definitely would apply to me currently. As stressed as I have been lately, I have an amazing life. I am going to correct this problem as soon as possible. Leaning on your loved ones for love and support helps me get through each day. If they only knew . . . which they NEVER will.

We have been back for a week now, and it was a needed break. All the teachers and students get refreshed, and now we can grind this out for the next ten weeks until spring break comes upon us. Luckily, there were not too many issues at school this week, just lots of paperwork, meetings, and phone calls? Have I said yet how cool it is to walk in and out of the classrooms while observing the interactions between my teachers and their students? Man, there is no other job like this! Believe it or not! The progress of the students you get to see throughout the year is awesome. My teachers are dedicated professionals who love children and want the best for them. It truly is awe-inspiring to watch a struggling student show so much growth from one year to the next.

How about a feel-good story? Who doesn't like one of those? I could write another book about what I see and observe on a daily basis regarding my students aged five to fourteen. At these ages in a school setting, most, if not all, just want to be loved, heard, and seen. This week, an issue happened with a fourth-grade student named Jules, which really isn't her name, but it is for the story. After you read this story, you will see why I didn't use her real name. Jules is a ten-year-old student who lives with her aunt and cousins. She has been attending Westmoreland school since the second grade. I haven't had too many problems with her, just small matters from time to time, nothing serious. Although today wasn't one of her better days. I know I said there were not too many issues at school this week, but thinking back, the situation with Jules wasn't a small predicament.

I was called on the radio by the custodian, Linda, that a student set a small fire in the girls' restroom by the gymnasium. When I arrived, a roll of toilet paper was smoldering. Fortunately, besides losing a roll of toilet paper and the bathroom smelling like smoke, nothing else had happened. The fire alarm didn't even go off! I was more concerned about that than trying to find out who did this dastardly deed. Fortunately, our school has cameras in the hallways, and the only student within the past twenty minutes that went into the bathroom was Jules. She and I had a good relationship, so I had hoped it wasn't her. Upon investigation, she admitted to doing it. Get this—her reason for setting the fire was attention seeking because, at home, she hasn't been getting any from her aunt, who works two jobs. When disciplining a student, I am not too harsh or strict. Setting a fire in the bathroom was a first for me, but I knew the punishment would have to be severe. Jules, sitting across from me at my desk, looked right at me and said something that startled me. It was also a first while disciplining a student. She cried, "Can you do me a favor and not call my aunt?" Obviously, I said no. She stammered, "Will you explain it all to her so she won't be mad at me?" I could have suspended her for quite a while, but I decided on just five days. Here is the kicker—her aunt told me they were moving, so I am losing one of my sheep. This is the life of an educator. I will leave it at that. I would make so many changes if I held a higher position in public education. DON'T GET ME STARTED!

Chapter 12

Call the Plumber

Sunday, January 28

Quote of the day: One of my good friends, Richard Nye, gets credit for this quote. I'm not sure where he got it from, to be quite honest. He has a good sense of humor and always has these one-liners that make you smile or laugh. One of his better sayings is "Don't play leapfrog with unicorns." I'm pretty sure that means, in life, when you take risks, be very careful.

My thought process last night kept me up most of the night thinking long-range of how in the world I am going to pay back $10,000 by the end of May. Sure, I still have four months, but as the saying goes, time flies! I haven't really had too many good ideas, and it isn't like I can ask anybody for advice since it is my secret. The other day, I stopped at the Shell gas station and decided to go in and get a couple of lottery tickets. And guess what? I WON! Hold on, hold on a minute. Slow your thinking down. Not enough to pay back what I owe. I still would be $9,980 short. Yes, I won twenty bucks! I have bought many lottery tickets in the past without much luck, so I'm fairly certain this is NOT the way to go. I might go further in the hole if I keep playing the lottery. It is kind of like playing the leapfrog game with unicorns. TOO RISKY!

Making things worse, I spent all day at school. Yes, on a Sunday. Doing paperwork? No! Preparing for meetings? Wrong again! Catching up on emails? I wish! How about I got a call from my custodian, Linda, at 7:18 this morning, frantically letting me know we had a pipe burst in one of the Special Education rooms.

Water was as far as you can see! The pipe must have burst the night before or maybe even earlier, especially if nobody came in the entire weekend to work in their classrooms to prepare for the week. Upon arrival, it was worse than I thought! Just a few weeks ago, there was a fire in the bathroom, and now a couple of my classrooms and an entire hallway are flooded. There was water everywhere! I had to call my boss, the superintendent, to let him know how bad it truly was. His name is Jack West. I will try to be as polite as possible describing him. Personally, I like Jack. He is an individual who doesn't smile much and has an opinion about everything. He expects A LOT and doesn't like excuses, which is something I can appreciate about him. Jack walked into the building and ambled down the hall in his rubber boots with a distasteful look on his mug. After he surveyed the catastrophe and talked to several people about what needed to be done, he actually stayed and helped out. After getting rid of the water and tearing up some old carpet, we sat down and developed a plan. Obviously, a couple of the rooms would have to be vacant for a week or two to repair the damages. We decided to move the Special Education class to the Music room. The other damaged room was a third-grade classroom, which will be moved to the Art room. The Art and Music teachers will be displaced for seven to fourteen days and will be traveling back and forth to the individual classrooms to provide instruction. Flexibility, patience, and problem-solving are life skills that we instill at school every day. I know the teachers and students will do their best during this time. They always do!

When I sat down with Jack, I wanted to share my problem (secret) with him and beg for forgiveness. But I just couldn't do it. He and I do not have that type of relationship. To be honest, I am certain he would not have taken it well. "Hey, Jack, is there any chance I can borrow $10,000 to replace the funds I stole from the rainy day account?"

I am home now after being at school from 7:30 AM to 6:30 PM. Poor Jenny, MJ, and Chloe don't get to see me too much through the week with my chaotic schedule. Now, on Sunday, we had plans to go to the movie theater; I had to tell them I am sorry I missed out on the family fun day. This is the part of my job that I loathe.

Chapter 13

Heart Attack

Friday, February 14

Quote of the day: Today's quote came from my pastor at church, Bill Pavlevich, who has been a dear friend of mine for many years. Not sure where he got this quote, or maybe he just came up with it himself. No matter, I need to repeat this quote over and over to myself: "When you start doubting yourself, remember how far you have come. Remember everything you have faced, all of the battles you have won, and all the fears you have overcome. Your greatest strength comes at your weakest days." Doesn't this sound like something a pastor would say when standing on the pulpit preaching to his congregation? If you said yes, good. If you said no, then go away. Just kidding! Please finish reading my story; you don't want to miss the ending. All books end with a happy ending, correct? Stay tuned. You might be surprised or even flabbergasted!

Obviously, as you can see by the date, today is Valentine's Day. If you asked my wife or polled a group of teachers, they would say this isn't one of their favorite days of the school year. It ranks right up there with Halloween and Picture Day as their least favorite days of the year. Why? Why, you say? If you are unsure, you must not have any friends who are teachers. Pure craziness! Check. Susie loves Joey! Check. Joey doesn't really like Susie! Check. Susie is unaware of this! She is nine years old. Check. Susie brings Joey a special card and chocolates! Check. Joey reluctantly brings Susie a bag of candy hearts. Check. Multiply this time one hundred different students around the school! Check. 100 Susies, and 100 Joeys! Check. Heart attack! Not for the students, mainly from the adults in the building, including yours truly. Normally, by the end of the day, one-half of the Susies are in tears because the Joeys are not paying attention to them at lunch recess. To be brutally honest, that is the way it should be. Susie shouldn't "love" Joey for a few more years yet. Not yet—you are too young! Deep down, I know it is all in good fun; however, when I got home today, I wanted to take a nap. Just like I do every year.

Something good did happen today, which might be a blessing from heaven. As a district, we are being required by the great state of South Carolina to have every student in our school write a story by the end of February. I get to pick the writing prompt for the entire district, which includes my school and five other schools, K-8. Having five- and six-year-olds write about the same prompt that thirteen and fourteen-year-olds are writing about seems silly to me, but that was not my decision. The kindergarten teacher will obviously help her students with the assignment compared to the eighth-grade teacher, who will NOT assist his or her students at all or at least very little. Here is the good news— no, the great news! My genius brain came up with this prompt. If you needed $10,000 to help your family pay off bills or a debt, how would you earn or raise enough money to do this? You are NOT allowed to borrow money from anybody or get the money illegally, like robbing a bank. Who knows? Kids do say—or in this instance, write down—the darndest things. All I need is ONE good suggestion to solve my problem. All of my worries could be over very shortly. Come on, Susie! Come on, Joey! Your principal needs your help. Sssshhhhh!

Chapter 14

Date Night

Sunday, February 23

Quote of the day: Oliver Wendell Holmes, who was a chief justice and associate justice on the Supreme Court in the early 1900s, said eloquently, "What lies behind us and what lies before us are tiny matters compared to what lies within us." Not only does this apply to me, but currently, this quote would also apply to my wife, Jenny. She is now four months pregnant. I feel like I have not really put much thought or effort into this pregnancy. I know I need to show Jenny more love and give her more of my attention. As of late, I have been crazy busy, somewhat selfish, and not honest. I need help. I need a miracle!

Knowing this, I have decided to write for another ten minutes since Jenny and the kids are at the mall, shoe shopping. I got out of this fun adventure because I just returned from school completing teacher evaluations. I was only three and a half weeks behind schedule on these. They are done, finally! I am going to write, shower, get dressed, and surprise Jenny and take her out for a romantic dinner at her favorite restaurant, Don Juan's Mexican Cantina. She deserves so much more, and I haven't been holding up my end of the bargain lately. Chicken nachos, chips, and salsa, and a large Diet Coke should be a good start to get me out of the doghouse. If I truly am in the doghouse, it is hard to tell sometimes because Jenny is so quiet and keeps her feelings inside. Now, it is after ten o'clock at night, and I have to say it was a delightful evening. Dinner was amazing, and we went for a stroll on the boardwalk by the beach. Why don't we do this more often? You want to know why? Because we are getting older and our jobs and kids tire us out by the end of each week. Not to mention cleaning the house, grocery shopping, laundry, etc. Excuses, excuses! We are no different than the typical American family. Our schedule is just as chaotic as everybody else's. We just need to make a commitment to each other that no matter what, we have a weekly date night or maybe monthly!

If only it was just that easy! It used to be before we had kids. Now, we are five months away from having another. The due date is July 15, which is actually fantastic because it is in the middle of the summer. Perfect timing for two adults whose careers are in education. I would take credit for that, but this pregnancy was not planned. Three years ago, I had a vasectomy. Now, I am very aware it did NOT work! Am I allowed to sue the doctor who did the procedure? Let's say for $10,000. I will have to look into this genius idea. Miracle? Ignorance?

Chapter 15

Leap Year

Friday, February 28

Quote of the day: "Patience and perseverance have a magical effect before which difficulties disappear and obstacles vanish" is a famous quote from our sixth president of the United States, John Quincy Adams. Adams was president from 1825 to 1829, and he is known for being the son of our second president, John Adams. He also helped to write the Monroe Doctrine. For the life of me, I can't remember what the Monroe Doctrine was about. I'm getting OLD, and my memory is fading. I called Jenny and told her I was going to be a little late coming home tonight. Several classes finished their writing prompts about how they would raise $10,000, so my plan is to skim through as many as I can and see if ONE or more can save my life from complete disaster.

I am assuming many of you that are reading this are saying, "Why doesn't the idiot finally just fess up and tell his wife that he messed up?" I have said that over and over to myself and have almost done that very same thing, but I know how my wife would react. It would not be pretty. I don't want to hurt her or have never trust me again, which is exactly what would happen. That is why it is called a secret. Of course, I feel like a loser, and I keep telling myself that once I get the debt paid back to the school, I will never, ever gamble again.

Reading over the prompts, I would like to share a few ideas that the students came up with using their imagination and child-like brains. How about the best ten ideas, in my opinion, going from 10 to 1? Keep in mind this year is a leap year, so I always think crazy things happen during this time. It's sort of like when a full moon comes out. Some of these ideas were way out there, and I knew they would be. I wouldn't want it any other way! I love reading students' stories!

> #10 Grade K: Lemonade stand ($10/person cup of lemonade) and one lotto ticket.
>
> #9 Grade 5: Garage sale, selling her three brothers' stuff since they don't take care of it.
>
> #8 Grade K: Buy 10 chickens, sell farm-fresh golden eggs.
>
> #7 Grade 6: Sell my dad's car; all he does is smoke in it, and my mom hates it.
>
> #6 Grade 1: Raffle off my dollhouse. I would sell between 100 and 1,000 raffle tickets.
>
> #5 Grade 7: Go metal detecting with my dad at the beach and find a rare coin.
>
> #4 Grade 2: Knock on the door of the richest guy in town and ask him nicely for money.
>
> #3 Grade 8: Write a letter to Tom Brady, ask for $10,000 because he can afford it.
>
> #2 Grade 4: My main man, Santa Claus, will help. Mail him a letter to the North Pole.

All are amazing ideas, and each one of them brought a HUGE smile to my face, which is just what I need right now. But, one idea seemed to stand out more than all of the others. If I had time to write a top 100 list, I would because there are so many more ideas that would crack you up or make you go, "What?" You might not agree with me, but I think this is something that might just work. Emma, a nine-year-old third-grade student, came up with this idea, and I personally love it.

> #1 Grade 3: Be a contestant on a game show like *Jeopardy*, *Wheel of Fortune*, or *The Price is Right*. My mom is smart, and I'm pretty sure she could win more than $10,000.

Hold on a minute, I'm smart! I've watched those shows before, and I think I would have a decent chance. In my opinion, my best chance would be the *Wheel of Fortune* since I am good at solving puzzles. It is a long shot, but it is something I am definitely going to research.

One more thing . . . I was talking about leap year and crazy things that happen. I have heard through a friend that something called the coronavirus that originated in China is spreading throughout the United States. I don't know too much about it yet, but I have a principals' meeting on Monday morning first thing to discuss it. An urgent email was sent out to all of the principals in my district late this afternoon that said the virus could get ugly. It can't be worse than the flu! Or can it? Argh!

Chapter 16

God Bless the USA

Monday, March 2

Quote of the day: Dale Carnegie, born in the late 1800s, had a famous quote that has always stuck with me. This is one I say to my children and the students at school who are struggling. "Most of the important things in the world have been accomplished by people who have kept on trying when there seemed to be no hope at all." Mr. Carnegie was a pioneer of self-improvement and a best-selling author in his day.

Unfortunately, my day started off badly, and it only got worse! Stupid leap year! That is past now, but this coronavirus is not. The experts are calling it COVID-19, and many are worried it is going to spread like wildfire in every community throughout the USA unless we start taking several precautions. The virus is VERY contagious and affects people who have respiratory issues. In a school setting where germs are rampant, especially this time of year, I am concerned!

I went to every classroom today and talked to each teacher and his or her students. My message focused on washing their hands often, sneezing and/or coughing into arms, and not touching each other if at all possible. Something called "social distancing" is being discussed, where you shouldn't be within six feet of another person and not congregating in groups of more than a certain number. No problem! Classrooms have anywhere from twenty to thirty students and are germ-infested no matter how well it is cleaned. I talked to the custodian, Linda, at length and came up with an action plan for the next month.

Doing some research, I discovered that this virus started on December 31, 2019, in Wuhan, China. Our president has now placed travel restrictions on people wanting or needing to leave or come into our country so the contagious virus would not spread. Just one week ago, he asked Congress to pass a 125-billion-dollar package for emergency funds to help fight this virus. A couple of days ago, on 2/28, a man from Seattle, Washington, who had been in Wuhan and came back home died from the virus to become the first man in the USA to perish from COVID-19. Some experts refute this, saying a man in California died from the virus on February 6. Internet! Geesssshhhh!

Sounds like this is something that is going to be an issue for quite a while. The unknown is scary for everybody, and I'm afraid that this might be just the beginning. Stay safe and follow the directions from the medical professionals who know a lot more about this than I do. More district meetings about COVID-19 are being discussed currently, so we can stay ahead of the game. As I write today's journal entry, I do not know of any reported cases of COVID-19 in South Carolina. Praise the Lord!

To make the day worse, if that is possible, this weekend, I looked into being on those three game shows to help me pay off my debt, and it is not going to happen. Why? Mainly because it takes months to even get a tryout to be on the shows, and that is if you can make it through the tryout round. You are put on a waiting list for up to a year or more. I have to pay off my debt by the end of the school year, which is the end of May. Such a great idea, but it is NOT going to happen because of time constraints. Bagwells NEVER quit! But I am close to tapping out!

Chapter 17

Out of Control

Thursday, March 12

Quote of the day: "If you have made mistakes, there is always another chance for you. You may have a fresh start any moment you choose, for this thing we call 'failure' is not the falling down but the staying down." This quote can be attributed to Mary Pickford, who was a silent film actress back in the early 1900s. She was known as America's Sweetheart and was one of the founders of the Oscar Awards.

Let's start this journal entry off with an update about the COVID-19 virus and where my school and community stand. Governor McMasters of our great state had a press conference on March 6 last week to let everybody know that the virus has reached South Carolina, declaring two women have tested positive. Since March 6, each day, more and more people are testing positive. The lack of tests, personal protective equipment (PPE), and ventilators necessary to fight this virus is not only a state issue but also a problem on the federal level. My nerves are at an all-time high.

Also, today after school, I learned that our school district is canceling all athletic functions, programs, and games until further notice. To top that, our school will be closed until March 31 and maybe longer. Wow! Mind-numbing! Chloe, who loves school, was upset because she had her first science fair tomorrow afternoon. Her classmates and teacher will have to wait to see what type of popcorn has the most kernels left after popping for two minutes each. Pssst . . . It is Jolly Time. Don't tell Chloe

I shared her conclusion. Her hypothesis was wrong, and she is still distraught about it. MJ seemed intrigued about not having to wake up everybody at 6:30 AM for the next couple of weeks, but baseball practice and games being canceled angered him beyond belief.

What I have heard and what is almost certain to happen is a statewide stay-at-home order being issued any day now. Life is about to change for everybody! I believe it is a good decision and makes complete sense to me. Why take any chances? Chloe can present her data to Jenny, MJ, and me in our living room regarding her experiment. MJ and I can play catch every day in the backyard to keep his arm in shape.

Plus, it will give Jenny a chance to relax and enjoy baby number 3 with a little help from yours truly. I am excited to announce we found out yesterday at her doctor's appointment that she is pregnant with a baby boy. Some day in mid-July, we will welcome Jacob Ryan Bagwell into the world. Two boys and one girl—Chloe is devastated! She wanted a baby sister so badly. MJ didn't seem to care one way or another. That is his personality. Although I think he wanted a brother . . . who knows?

I guess, from time to time, I will go to work and get some things done. Jenny can work in her classroom while the kids can play in the gym. The kids love coming to the school with us. Who would think that? I would have loved this, too, as a kid. Playing in the gym for one to three hours is not a bad deal, especially for somebody who loves sports like I used to way back when. I need to call Jack, my boss, to see if this is even possible. I haven't heard yet whether or not the school building is closed to employees too. Stay-at-home order? All day? Is the country shutting down completely?

Chapter 18

The Governor Has Spoken

Tuesday, March 24

Quote of the day: Here is a name that you probably might not know: Saint Francis de Sales. Back in the 1500s, he was known as the Gentleman Saint and was a bishop of Geneva. Is it a famous quote if a person has never heard of him? Hmm . . . "Be patient with all things, but first with yourself. Never confuse your mistakes with your value as a human being. You are a perfectly valuable, creative, worthwhile person simply because you exist. And, no amount of triumphs or tribulations can ever change that." I need to put this on a piece of colored paper and frame it to put on my wall at school in my office. When a student is having a bad day, he or she and I can read this quote together and discuss it in depth. Saint Francis backs that quote up with this shorter one: "Be who you are AND be that WELL." Yes, amen!

Did you hear last week on televisions, or maybe you read about it online, that now all fifty states have the coronavirus present? I still am having a hard time wrapping my finger around this. The outbreak is being labeled as a pandemic worldwide. It is affecting millions and killing thousands upon thousands. What kind of beast is this, and how do we tame it?

Today, Governor McMasters had another press conference stating that all schools now are closed until May 1. The $10,000 debt that I incurred is the furthest thing on my mind right now. Personally, as I write this entry tonight, I do not know anyone here locally that has tested positive for COVID-19, nor do I have any family members around the country that have been stricken by the virus. I pray at least twice a day for everybody to remain healthy and safe. I am asking you to do the same.

All we see on the news 24/7 is about this virus. I have so many questions and concerns that I feel needed to be answered, but I am not sure even the doctors are 100 percent certain about some of this. How scary is that? I'm trying not to think about it all day long. Jenny is the worrywart in the family, so that is her job. My plan is to spend time with the kids and Jenny while we have some downtime.

Don't judge me after you read this paragraph. Or, in reality, I guess you can because I don't know you, so it won't hurt my feelings any. This past Saturday night, I made the executive decision that we were going to "get out" of the house and go to the McDonald's drive-thru for supper. McDonald's! I haven't eaten dinner there in many, many years. The chicken nuggets aren't as good as I remember them being when I was in college. What happened? The next night, I picked up pizza and wings and Pizza Hut. Somewhat better! Still not worth the $23 I spent, but the kids were thrilled, and so was Jenny, who didn't have to cook. I DON'T COOK, BY THE WAY! GREASE FIRE 2012, enough said! Yesterday, it was Icee's at the gas stations. Fast food, pizza, and Icee's back-to-back-to-back days. Why not, right? Tonight, I did cook—frozen pizza. Pizza, again? Don't judge me! LOL. WE have all been there. Tomorrow, Hot Pockets? Say it ain't so!

Chapter 19

April Fools #1

Quote of the day: "I've learned that people will forget what you said, people will forget what you did, but people will never forget how you made them feel" (Maya Angelou). She was born in 1928 and became a well-known poet, author, and singer. She was a civil rights activist and opened doors for African Americans, especially females who were aspiring to become authors. I love researching influential Americans and seeing their accomplishments. A true inspiration for all of us to look up to and aspire to be.

Bad News (Part I): I heard on the local news last night that forty-six counties in South Carolina have reported at least one positive case of the coronavirus. The number of positive cases on some days is doubling from the day before. You think 1,200 positive cases on Tuesday was a lot, then you hear Wednesday night there are 2,400-plus new cases. Twenty-four hours later, it doubled! Yikes! Ouch! Wow! Gadzooks! I'm depressed and feeling more melancholy by the day. Then, this bombshell hit me.

Bad News (Part II): I also received an email from my boss that the district is coming to all the schools and will be doing some end-of-the-year accounting paperwork. Word has it that we will NOT be going back to school for the rest of the year, but that decision won't be made for two to three weeks yet. There is only a 1 percent chance that we come back, according to Jack. This isn't bad news; it is horrific news! I did not sleep a wink last night.

Do you think Jack was pulling my leg in his email? It was April 1 yesterday. I have been working from home this whole week. I would think I should go into school if they were indeed planning on tidying up the accounts on my hard drive and on my computer. Jack is not one to play tricks, so I know that he was serious. This, most likely, leaves me today, tomorrow, and the weekend to scrounge up $10,000. No problem! Do you think Santa Claus is available at the North Pole if I can find him? I need an early Christmas present.

Chapter 20

April Fools #2

Obviously, I knew Jack wasn't joking in his email. It was just wishful thinking on my part. I have to share this story with you. I need to smile right now since my insides are turning, thinking about the inevitable. This is something that happened while I was teaching many years ago. I was a sixth-grade teacher for a few years before I became a principal. My brain comes up with some good ideas from time to time; this was not one of them. It was in my first year of teaching, so we can blame it on my young age back when I used to be cool. Boy, times have changed!

People who know me well would tell you that I joke around a lot and like to tease. It was mid-March, and I noticed on the calendar that after we get back from spring break, it would be April 1. I thought, bingo! I am going to do an April Fools' Day joke on my students in my class. This will be revenge on them for all the talking they did throughout the entire year. Let's just say they were a chatty group who would get an A+ on their communication skills. BUT deep down, I absolutely loved each and every one of them. It was my first year of teaching, like I said. You always want your calls to be the best they can be, and as a first-year teacher, you strive to make each day "fun" if possible. You are young and have lots of energy. I thought and thought for many days about what I could pull off to not only fool them but really make it memorable. Not sure where I finally came up with this idea, but all I can say is I am creative and imaginative.

My prank needed reinforcements to make this happen. I talked to a permanent substitute teacher who floats from room to room, helping teachers with various tasks. She was getting ready to leave for spring break when I stopped her in the hallway. I shared with her that I needed her to come to my class on Monday morning when we get back from spring break. She would read a letter that I wrote to my student once the announcements were over at 8:25 AM. I would be in the conference room, hiding, so the student did not see me. The letter stated that I was fired due to insufficient funds, and the school district had to terminate the contracts of all first-year teachers. It also mentioned that I moved to Florida and I would try to visit on the last day of school. Also, their new teacher would start the next day on April 2, and she was a retired warden from a prison. I guess I went a little overboard, just a little! My class had music class at 8:30 AM every Monday morning, so my plan was to be sitting in the music room when they walked in with the permanent sub and shout, "April Fools!"

I forgot one important thing about this joke. My class and I were very close and had a strong bond. The permanent sub called the office at 8:27 AM and quietly asked for me so the students didn't hear her inquiring about my whereabouts. The secretary beckoned me over behind her desk, and when I asked her what was going on, she responded she had just finished reading the letter, and ALL twenty-three students were crying. She said I might want to come down to the classroom immediately and tell them that it was just a joke.

The music teacher, Ms. Barone, was in the office and heard about what was happening. She wanted to come down to my classroom with me. I asked her to walk in first, then come back out and tell me how bad it was. She reluctantly agreed, and thirty seconds later, she sauntered out with a sheepish look on her face. She said what the permanent sub told me. All of the students were teary-eyed and /or crying. I stood frozen, feeling awful that my joke backfired miserably. Left . . . right . . . left . . . right! Come on, feet, move! I tiptoed in the back door, and all I could think to say was "Guys, what's wrong? April Fools!" For what felt like a minute (but in reality, it was probably seven or eight seconds), not one student said a word. It was like they were seeing a ghost!

Especially because they thought I was in Florida, not South Carolina. Then, out of nowhere, one of my students, a girl named Lori, cried out, "That was the meanest, cruelest joke anybody has ever played on me!" That broke the stillness, and each and every one of them vowed revenge on me. Memorable, YES! Yes times a hundred! This was my best April Fools' joke I have ever pulled off. To this day, I look back on it with a smile. Mean, Mr. Bagwell. ☺

Chapter 21

It Is Time to Pay the Piper

Sunday, April 5

Quote of the day: Henry Ford, born in 1863 and founder of the Ford Motor Company, gets credit for this quote. "Whether you think you can or you think you can't, you're right." Truth hurts with this saying. Mr. Ford, who probably is most famous for his Model T car or starting assembly lines for mass production, was an intelligent man. His quotes hit home with me. I love reading about him and his way of thinking, especially from somebody who lived so long ago.

Tomorrow is the big day! I am planning on heading to the bank to either withdraw $10,000 from my savings account or get a loan from the bank manager. If I get a loan, I have to pay back the entire sum in six months so that I am not charged any interest. Honestly, I am not sure what I am going to do yet. It is imperative I get the money to put back into the rainy day account before Ms. Reilly, the accountant, shows up to do the books.

My plan is to get up early and be the first person at the bank. Due to the COVID-19, my bank has only drive-up or drive-thru service (whatever you call it), where you pull up to the doohickey cylinder that travels through a tube to the teller. Both MJ and Chloe want to come because they know they will get a Dum Dums sucker from the teller at 8:30 in the morning. Sugar! If I were them, I would rather sleep in and not get up. Of course, they also know I will take them to McDonald's for breakfast or Dunkin' Donuts after I complete my banking business. Dad is a sucker!

Luckily, all I have to do is transfer the money from my account into the school's rainy day account. My personal account and the school both do business at the same bank, which has a branch right down the street from my house. Sweet! Community National Bank is a friendly, helpful bank that my family has used for many, many years. All the tellers, thankfully, are younger and must not have any children of their own because they know me as Mr. Bagwell, not Principal Bagwell.

It is MJ's thirteenth birthday today, so I am going to surprise him and take him fishing at the lake. MJ loves to fish even though he rarely catches anything. Although, two years ago, he hooked a baby shark, which not only fascinated him but startled him as well. MJ HATES sharks. Despises them! Not sure why. It must be from me making him watch Jaws ever since he was five years old. Oops! My bad! Jenny tried to warn me, but I didn't listen. What?

If you are wondering, MJ's initials stand for Michael Jordan. Jenny reluctantly agreed to this name for our firstborn. She didn't necessarily like the name Michael. After much discussion, we decided on MJ for short. Jenny is not athletic and doesn't like sports much at all. On the other hand, I grew up a big Chicago Bulls fan, especially in the 1980s, when Michael Jordan started to become a superstar. His sister, Chloe, was almost named CJ, but at the last second, we mutually agreed that Chloe sounds better. I have a bad feeling that baby Jacob is going to be spoiled big time by both his brother and sister. And Mom . . . okay, and me! Sorry! Not really! I'm like a big kid. Ask Jenny! Actually, don't.

Chapter 22

Why Me?

Wednesday, April 22

Quote of the day: This is my last quote of the day, and you will find out why when you keep reading this chapter. I apologize now for not knowing who is responsible for this quote. "Sometimes you must hurt in order to know, fall in order to grow, lose in order to gain, because most of life's greatest lessons are learned through pain." You can say throughout this whole ordeal of keeping this secret to myself that I have learned a lesson. The struggle was real, and I was in a lot of pain, and now the pain can't be more intense! Or can it? Keep reading.

Have you noticed by now that I say "Why me?" a lot? For a good reason this time. I haven't written in my journal for seventeen days. Seventeen! Where have I been? What have I been doing? Why me? Why me? Why me? Jenny dislikes that I say this phrase over and over. She says "I'm sorry" ten times per day, so why can't I say "Why me?" ten times per day?

After I finished my last journal entry on April 5, I received a call from my boss, Jack, letting me know that I needed to come into the Admin building the next morning at 7:30 AM for an urgent meeting. He wouldn't tell me over the phone, but I was almost certain that I know what it was about. The cancellation of school for the remainder of the year was my guess. The question was, how in the world will we make this work? There is something that our district has, and it is called e-learning, where the students can do work from their house via their iPads. A lot of planning is involved to pull this off. The students have already been doing this every Monday, Wednesday, and Friday. Sooooooo . . . I was half right! School has been canceled for the remainder of the year. This was made official not by Jack but by the governor himself. We will continue doing e-learning until the end of May. Under the circumstances, there really wasn't a choice any other way. A lost year . . . almost!

Going back to the last time I wrote on April 5, I was going to the bank the next morning to transfer the money from my account to the school account. Getting Jack's phone call, I knew that my trip to the bank would be slightly delayed until our meeting finished. MJ and Chloe were bummed! No breakfast at McDonald's or donuts with Dad. No suckers from the drive-thru at the bank. Crushing news to a kid!

Something happened that night, or should I say in the middle of the night. I woke up sweating and short of breath, which really isn't that unusual as of late. This time just felt different in some way. I can't really explain it. It was time! I needed to tell Jenny what was going on for the past several months. My secret! I'm tired of living a lie, and Jenny deserves better. Why didn't I do this sooner? In reality, nothing has changed this whole time regarding my debt. I am right back where I started when I lost the money betting on the football games. My brain kept telling me that I would get out of this somehow, someway without getting caught. Not only was I being distrustful of my wife, but I STOLE money from my workplace. How low can a person get in his life? People from my community revere me, and unbeknownst to them, I am a low-life.

Waking up Jenny at 2:45 AM, if I recollect, she woke up groggily from a deep sleep, trying to figure out why I was whispering her name with tears rolling down my cheeks. I remember exactly what she said: "Nyles, what is wrong? You are scaring me! What is it?"

Trying to hold back the tears and stop shaking uncontrollably, I cried, "I am a piece of crap! I have been holding back a secret from you for months because I didn't want to hurt you."

Jenny retorted, "Whatever it is, we will work through it, and you aren't a piece of crap!"

That's funny, I thought sarcastically to myself. I sure feel like one and have felt this way for some time. How about a loser if I am not a piece of crap? Worthless? Ignorant? Pathetic? Where is the thesaurus when I need it? Somebody look up the word stupid, and all the synonyms would apply to me. How could I have let it go this far? We talked for almost an hour, mainly me just apologizing over and over to her, asking for her forgiveness. It was my turn to say her favorite phrase, "I'm sorry!" She took it better than I thought, but she was extremely concerned about me taking the money to cover the debt from the school account more than the fact that I lost the $10,000. I told her of my plan of going to the bank and transferring the money after my meeting with Jack. She was relieved to hear this and, through clenched teeth, said we will finish this discussion at some point after I get back from the meeting and the bank. When she said, "On your way home, make sure you pick up a dozen donuts," a huge burden just unclenched its grip from my chest. I actually started giggling and couldn't stop for two minutes. It felt good to actually laugh. Lately, my smiles have been fake and forced. I'm free! At least, I was for a couple of hours until this bombshell hit. What now? Chapter 23's title might be a good hint.

Chapter 23

Detective Jackson

Thursday, April 23

I was going to finish writing what happened when I woke up the next day and had to go to the meeting and the bank, but I was interrupted by MJ and Chloe, who wanted to spend time with their grieving father. Grieving? Yes! I woke up very exhausted from not getting much sleep the night before and showered, dressed, and had a cup of coffee to go. Driving up to the Admin building, I was three minutes early, which is pretty remarkable for me. Yep, I am one of those people who are always late and make others wait. Drives poor Jenny crazy!

I don't even know how to put into words what happened next, but I will try. Close your eyes and try to picture this scene. Greeted by Jack's secretary, she led me into his office, where I noticed Jack, Riley Reilly, and a man who I, minutes later, found out was Detective William Jackson. A lump formed in my throat, my stomach became nauseous instantaneously, and I sat down uneasily at the head of the table with six eyes glaring in my direction.

First to talk was Detective Jackson, who introduced himself and said that he wanted to ask me a couple of questions. He mentioned that I did not have to answer the questions if I didn't want to, but I froze and blurted out that he could ask me anything he wanted, which, in hindsight, was a BIG mistake, and I should have known better. I should have said to direct all of his questions to my attorney. Since I don't have an attorney, my mind didn't think of this possibility. My brain does not like to work under pressure, I guess. You think with all of my experience as a principal, I could talk my way out of anything. "Fire away," I said. To my dismay, he obviously peppered me with several questions regarding missing funds from multiple accounts at the school. I tried to soften the blow and be honest about the $10,000 from the rainy day account, but I was clueless regarding any other misappropriations during my tenure at Westmoreland.

Jack seemed nervous and uneasy; he almost looked like he felt sorry for me and didn't know what to say. I swear, at one point during the meeting, or should I call it an interrogation, that his voice cracked and his eyes were moist. I somehow held it together and did not shed a tear, which is kind of surprising. The tear ducts must have dried up because of all the crying I have been doing for many months. As I sat there and listened intently, all I could think about was my pregnant wife and two kids. At one point, I remember asking Detective Jackson to repeat his question because my mind was on my family, and I didn't hear a word he said. Ms. Reilly, on the other hand, just sat there, uncomfortably moving from side to side, taking notes on her legal pad of paper.

I was told that I was not being detained or, worse yet, arrested as of right now. It was an open investigation, and I was placed on paid leave until further notice. Unsteadily, I chose to shake everybody's hand and ambled out to my parked car. I was open to suggestions about how in the world I was going to tell Jenny what had just happened. One thing for sure—I don't need to go to the bank now. McDonald's, here I come. Four number 10 combo meals to go. Supersize, PLEASE!

Chapter 24

O' Happy Birth

Saturday, April 25

Yes, today is my birthday. Actually, it is my big 5-0! Didn't really feel like celebrating, so I did my best to keep a smile on my face for an unsuspecting MJ and Chloe, who have NO idea what is going on currently. Jenny was a whirlwind of emotions. As I write tonight, I am pretty sure she has used all of them. Anger and sadness being the top two. She has every right to show both of these. I am not making any excuses for my behavior. We talked and had a heartfelt conversation about the present and the foreseeable future. Many ideas were bantered back and forth—some positive and some negative, or should I say brutally honest. The important thing is I have a meeting on Monday morning with an attorney whom my next-door neighbor knows really well and recommended.

Talking about my next-door neighbor, my kids spent the entire day over there from 8:00 AM to 5:00 PM. My birthday dinner was planned for 6:00 PM, so Jenny and I spent all day outside cleaning the garage and the yard. Then, we ventured out to the grocery store, wearing our masks and trying to stay six feet away from others the best we could. As we shopped for essentials, we noticed that some of the things we needed weren't even on the shelves due to the COVID-19 supply-and-demand crisis. Steaks, rolls, lettuce, and ice cream were no problem. Toilet paper was nowhere in sight! Toilet paper . . . toilet paper . . . if you only knew!

We pulled into our garage at 4:12 PM, and I carried in

most of the groceries while Jenny was on her phone, talking to her mom about COVID-19. I went back out to the garage to get two large bags of salt pellets for the water softener when Jenny came sprinting out, crying about something. She mumbled a few things, but I could not understand what she was trying to convey. Catching her breath, she stammered, "I smell gas!"

Slowly, I walked back inside to see—or should I say smell—what Jenny did. At first, I thought she was crazy because I didn't smell a thing. She was close on my heels when she nudged me to the back of the house, and then I, too, smelled the rancid odor. She and I went back toward the kitchen, and she was trying to take charge and come up with what we should do or, in other words, the correct protocol.

She said that we need to go outside and call the gas company so they can come to check for "the leak." I told her to wait a minute and let me investigate a little further. She scolded me for staying in the house. I felt like a puppy who just had an accident. She stomped away and went out the front door while I headed back to where I thought the smell was originating. Passing the closet where the gas furnace was located kind of surprised me because that is where I had a good idea I would be going to find the stench. BUT the smell was coming from the kids' bathroom, and as I tiptoed in there, a sly smile came to my face as I looked down and noticed what was in the toilet. As I held my nose with one hand, I flushed the toilet with the other hand—twice! I didn't know whether to laugh or be angry. MJ forgets to flush, and I'm fairly certain this will be the last time he forgets.

Walking toward the door to go find Jenny and share what I found, I noticed she was on the phone AGAIN. I assumed she was talking to her mom, but she was talking to the gas company. Interrupting her as fast as I could, she told the natural gas representative on the phone to please hold since she couldn't hear what I was trying to tell her. After I told her that it wasn't a gas leak but an "MJ moment," she did her best to tell the representative on the phone what it actually was. How embarrassing, right? She was told that, since she called and reported a leak, they still had to come out and make sure. I repeat: how embarrassing, right? O' happy birth, o' happy birth, o' happy birthday to me! They did show up rather quickly and did a thorough check of the entire house. I refused to go in and be a part of it. Jenny called. She didn't listen to me and called anyway, so Jenny had to do the walk of shame with the man from the gas company. One thing is for certain—I sure won't ever forget my fiftieth birthday.

Chapter 25

Truth Hurts

Monday, April 27

My meeting with the lawyer today was interesting, to say the least. Other adjectives that might describe the meeting would be *informative, nerve-racking,* and *downright scary*. Here is what I learned. The crime I committed would be a felony in the state of South Carolina. It is a white-collar crime called embezzlement because I was employed at a corporation or business that includes schools. Also, it could be categorized as financial identity fraud when somebody (me) appropriated financial resources belonging to someone else and used those resources as their (mine) own. Most importantly, in legal terms, it is a breach of trust—basically, someone trusting you to deal with a certain amount of money for a specific reason and using it without their permission for another reason. What an eye-opening, jaw-dropping day!

The maximum time sentenced for the amount of money I took would be up to ten years, and I would likely be levied a large fine, which is up to the judge's discretion. The fine I would have no problem paying; however, ten years locked up at the state prison would be a nightmare. Just so you know, I have never been in trouble my entire life, not even a parking ticket. My lawyer told me, since I have never been in any legal trouble, that will be a huge benefit for me. I need all the help I can get!

Jenny went with me, and for this, I could not thank her enough. She is dealing with the situation the best she can. I feel like a complete bum knowing she has my back, yet she doesn't deserve this, especially this late into her pregnancy. We still have not told MJ and Chloe about any of this. I know the time will come when we need to sit down with both of them and explain the situation. If I do indeed get arrested, which my lawyer says is likely, then I will most likely be on the front page of the newspaper. Why me? My lawyer was NOT at all happy with me when I told him I had talked to a detective about the missing money. Looking back on it, I should not have signed the papers giving permission for him to question me. He had a search warrant in his possession to search through my office and all of my technology, including my phone, laptop, and computer. I panicked, thinking I could talk my way out of it with just a slap on the wrist. Not likely then and even more unlikely now!

The drive back to the house was extremely quiet, and my whole body was numb. The lawyer is going to have me come back for another meeting next Monday to discuss what might happen in the next week or two. My lawyer's name is Bart Reynolds . . . no, not Burt Reynolds, Bart Reynolds. I almost forced a slight smile the first time I heard his name, but I haven't been in a laughing mood as of late, nor will I be anytime soon! Like I said, my whole body is NUMB!

Chapter 26

Power of Prayer

Wednesday, April 29

After Wednesday night's church service, I decided I needed to talk about my situation to somebody that I trusted and knew he would be there for me no matter what. That person was Pastor Pavlevich, whom I have always looked up to. I should have talked to him before, and I think I mentioned in a previous journal entry I wanted to, but I didn't for one reason or another. We had a lengthy discussion, which I sorely appreciated, and he urged me to pray about this for some inner peace. I love quotes of the day and top ten lists, so I think there is no better time than now to break out my top ten favorite Bible verses. If you have not made a list of your favorite verses, I highly recommend you do. It brings a smile to your face and also just makes you feel good about yourself. When I read my list, it makes me want to go out and help others. Write a letter to a friend you haven't spoken to in a while, send an email to somebody you are close to and tell him or her what you appreciated about them, or help out your elderly neighbor who can't get around like they used to are great examples of WWJWYTD ("What would Jesus want you to do?"). Maybe some of my favorite verses are some of your favorites as well. Writing helps me unwind during this low time in my life. But please be aware of this—I am going to fight this and not feel sorry for my shortcomings. Nobody is perfect like Pastor Pavlevich preached to me tonight. Jesus does forgive our sins if we repent of them. I am going to renew my spiritual faith tonight and give him all the glory going forward.

I hope you enjoy reading these as much as I enjoy writing them for your viewing pleasure. In order 1 to 10:

1. "I can do all things through Christ who strengthens me." (Philippians 4:13)
2. "I am with you always, even to the end." (Matthew 28:20)
3. "For God so loved the world that he gave His only begotten son, that whoever believes in Him should not perish but have everlasting life." (John 3:16)
4. "It is God who arms me with strength, and makes my way perfect." (Psalm 18:32)
5. "But those who wait on the Lord shall renew their strength; they shall mount up with wings like eagles, they shall run and not be weary, they shall walk and not faint." (Isaiah 40:31)
6. "Therefore, my beloved brethren, be steadfast, immovable, always abounding in the work of the Lord, knowing that your labor is not in vain in the Lord." (1 Corinthians 15:58)
7. "If God is for us, who can be against us?" (Romans 8:31)
8. "Pleasant words are like a honeycomb, sweetness to the soul and health to the bones." (Proverbs 16:24)
9. "And we have known and believed the love that God has for us. God is love, and he who abides in love abides in God, and God in him." (1 John 4:16)
10. "Behold, I am with you and will keep you wherever you go, and will bring you back to this land; for I will not leave you until I have done what I have spoken to you." (Genesis 28:15)

Wow! I feel like singing a song or two after I reread what verses I just wrote. My favorite Christian hymn is "The Old Rugged Cross." I can almost hear you humming, whistling, or quietly singing the first verse because I know I am. Are any of the top ten verses that I picked similar to a list you might make?

I would guess a couple similarities would exist. The stress I am now under is something I can't even describe in words. Literally, I could go from the peak of the mountains to the bottom of the sea in a snap. Not something I like to think of, but I have to be realistic. I'm praying daily for guidance from my lawyers, sympathy from others if this case becomes public, and forgiveness from my wife, Jenny. I just prayed right now after writing this journal entry. I prayed that I did not want to take any of his blessings for granted. Being able to talk to the Lord is a privilege. In Him, I can and will find the strength to endure. His steadying hands will protect me. In His name, amen! I might not need a miracle, but I will take one if He deems it so. Also, pray for the people who have contacted the coronavirus. I heard a few days ago almost 5,000 people in South Carolina have tested positive. Our stay-at-home order has been extended, and I agree 100 percent.

Chapter 27

Cell 108

Friday, May 1

This morning, I woke up to birds chirping, wind blowing, and the sun shining. Sounds like a good start to hopefully a great day ahead. Well, let me tell you what happened today. It is now 10:11 PM, and luckily, I will be lying in my bed to go to sleep here pretty soon. Jenny is already asleep, thankfully! Her day was almost as stressful as my day.

Getting ready to take a shower this morning at 8:11 AM, my cell phone rang, and I did not answer it because I did not recognize the number on the Caller ID. Two minutes later, it rang again, coming from the exact same number. No voicemails were left, so I was assuming it wasn't that important. Undressing, almost walking to the bathroom, the phone rang again. My ringtone is "Go, Cubs, Go," and it is very catchy. I love to hear it over and over, but three times in five minutes was enough.

Answering abruptly and impatiently, I sarcastically did not say hello; instead, I just said yes. There was a brief pause before a man said, "Is this Nyles Bagwell?" I retorted back, "Yes, this sure is." To my dismay, it was Detective Jackson, and he let me know that he needed me to step outside because he had a warrant for my arrest. Many emotions started racing through my body, and I tried to politely tell him that I wasn't even dressed. He told me to get dressed but not to hang up and then walk out my front door in the next minute with my hands held high in the air. Wow, I thought. I am not a criminal, or I didn't consider myself one even though I broke the law. The longer I thought about it, I know that he was just following protocol and procedure. A true walk of shame. Luckily, the kids were asleep, and I had just enough time to tell Jenny that she would need to go to the bank or the bail bond building and see how much she needed to withdraw to get me out ASAP. I was hoping I would be in and out in ten minutes, but it doesn't always work out the way you want it.

The ride in the police car couldn't have been more embarrassing, and I was mortified beyond belief. The ride took approximately ten minutes, but it seemed much longer. Not that you should be surprised, but you would be right that I have NEVER been in the back of a police car. Let me tell you something—it is extremely uncomfortable, and the handcuffs were so tight. All I can remember is that I did not say a word to the officer who was driving, and he was listening to a classic rock station on the radio. It seemed rather loud. I thought about telling him to lower the volume, but I didn't for some reason. Probably because I knew he wouldn't turn it down for the reason he didn't care about how bad my head hurt from worrying about what was about to happen.

Arriving at the jail, my first thought was to get the handcuffs off that were strangling the blood circulation in my wrists. Trying to describe how uncomfortable it is to have handcuffs on wouldn't do them justice on how bad it truly felt. Walking slowly inside the jail and having the cuffs removed truly was a relief. This just happened eleven hours ago, so I should remember all of the details of what transpired next, but it was a blur and something I never want to relive.

The normal things happened, you might guess. I had to undress to be searched for weapons or contraband before I was given a set of jail clothes to put on with a pair of generic Crocs that looked like they had been worn by one thousand people before me. Even though I had been searched, I still had to be body-scanned by an expensive X-ray machine. Furthermore, I was then led to a room that I do remember was cell number 108. I would call it not really a waiting room so much but more of a holding cell for inmates waiting to talk to an officer and answer the fifty questions he or she would have for me. Waiting room— really, Nyles!

Answering the basic questions that the officer asked, I was

indeed allowed to make a phone call. I chose to call Jenny, of course, to see where she was. She mentioned that she was about ready to leave the house and head to the bail bondsman. Detective Jackson stayed after I got whisked away in the police car and talked to Jenny for five to ten minutes, letting her know what was going to happen next. He shared with her that I had four felony charges against me for embezzlement and fraud. My bond was for a $10,000 cash bond and $5,000 for a surety bond.

While I was sitting in the holding cell for quite a while before I was called out, not too much happened that was interesting or even strange. One other inmate was in the holding cell when I got there, but he was sleeping. My best-guess scenario would be that I was in there for two hours before another officer came and got me to take my mug shot and fingerprints. I inquired about whether or not my wife had been there yet to bail me out. He seemed confused about my question because I never got a straight answer from him. Not knowing what would happen next, I started to become anxious and just a touch nervous. I did NOT want to be placed in an actual cell with another inmate—or should I say prisoner. Not sure what you are called when you are in county jail. A loser? Maybe not everybody, but I sure felt like one.

The officer did place me back in the holding cell to my relief and said he found out that my wife was indeed there, and I would be released shortly. Whew, great news, I thought! It still took another hour, maybe even two hours, before I could walk out of jail feeling a sense of relief in every pore of my body. Several people came in and out during the three to four hours I was in the holding cell, especially toward the end. The most interesting person was a man I met whose name I did not get, nor did I really care, to be honest. He told me that he was arrested on a theft charge, but he gave his twin brother's name to the officer when he got arrested. He was worried that when they took his fingerprints, they would soon discover he had lied about who he really was. Then they would give him another charge. Well, duh! Jenny driving me out of the parking lot and back toward the house was relieving even though I knew I had a lot of explaining and apologizing to do.

Chapter 28

You're Fired!

Monday, May 4

The quote "Life is 10 percent of what happened to you and 90 percent of how you react to it" makes complete sense to me. Man, my reaction to this disaster is pure grief. Yes, as you can tell by the chapter's title, I did lose my job. I had a letter delivered to me from the school corporation this morning around 11:30 AM. That didn't take long, I thought. Since I was already on the six-o'clock and the ten-o'clock news for getting arrested, Jenny and I had to sit down with MJ and Chloe and tell them what is currently happening. A reporter has already come to our house and asked if I wanted to comment on my arrest. The sad look on the kids' faces was almost worse than my brief jail experience.

Trying to stay positive and remembering that our Lord Jesus Christ is always there for me to lean on is the only way I am still functioning. I am a mess, Jenny and the kids are a mess, and our lives will no longer EVER be the same. That is a tough pill to swallow. My parents are driving up from Florida, and my sister is flying in from Colorado for moral support and to help take care of the kids. What a blessing!

I had my second meeting with my lawyer at two this afternoon. He obviously knew about my arrest, and it came a little earlier than he had even expected. He is almost too honest when he shares information and his legal advice regarding what might happen next with my case. Deep down, it hurts to hear the truth and know that I could be in BIG trouble, depending on how far Detective Jackson and the prosecutor want to go. My lawyer's concern is not only the money I stole that I admitted to taking but the other three felonies that were charged against me. I had to be upfront and honest with him, so I decided to just throw it all out on the table. My secret that I shared with you about me borrowing money from the rainy day account wasn't the whole story. I have a bigger secret that I haven't shared with you (or anybody else) until today when I told my lawyer. Gulp! My real secret is . . .

Chapter 29

I Am an Addict

Thursday, May 7

The last couple of days have been almost too much to handle. Luckily (or should I say fortunately), my parents have arrived, and my sister should be here within the hours. My dad, MJ, and Chloe went to pick her up at the airport. The support I am getting from my family is truly inspirational. My plan is to sit down with everybody tomorrow morning or early afternoon and come forward with the declaration of having a gambling addiction and I need help. Hello, my name is Nyles, and I have a gambling problem. My lawyer said I should start going to Gamblers Anonymous meetings for counseling sessions, whatever they are called. He mentioned that it would look good to the judge that I have made an effort.

The first step to getting help is to admit you have a problem. Well, that time is now, and it hurts something crazy to tell your loved ones about a problem that you have kept secret.

Jenny and I have not really had a long, one-on-one, exhaustive talk yet. We have had a few short discussions, but nothing like we need to have. Looking ahead, Jenny is going to deliver baby Jacob in two short months, and at her age, I worry about complications. Adding to her stress level because of my issues hurts deeply. If I am convicted and have to serve time in prison, what happens? Can she raise three kids as a single mom with a career without me and my income? It won't be easy, that is for sure! The other thing we haven't talked about is, do I plead guilty and do a plea agreement or go to trial and hope for the best? My lawyer and I briefly discussed this, but the prosecutor has not even presented a plea deal yet. That is down the road. We are not talking a week or two for this process. My lawyer said this most likely will stretch out between two and four months. Living in fear of the unknown is not a good feeling whatsoever. Unfortunately, Jenny is going through the same thing. I am picturing in my head the movie Rocky II and the character Adrian. She was pregnant in the movie and didn't want Rocky to fight. Rocky did not listen to her. This caused A LOT of stress, and eventually, she ended up in the hospital. Let's be realistic—Jenny is forty-four years old and internalizes her stress. Now is not the time to do this. It is not healthy! She knows, and I know, but the situation is almost too much.

Tucking the kids into bed was something that I take for granted. Tonight and every night forthcoming, I plan to sit on the edge of the bed and talk to both of them for a couple of minutes, sharing a fun memory from the past or anything else they want to talk about. My sister should be here any minute, so I am going to end here. Hopefully, her plane was on time, and there wasn't a delay. I think I will go call her cell phone to see where they are at and how much longer until they arrive. Never mind, I just heard the front door open. MJ is running through the house and up the stairs, bellowing, "I need to pee!" Bye, bye!

Chapter 30

Mother's Day

Sunday, May 10

Not only are we going to spoil Jenny today, but my mother and sister are in town. A three-for-one special, which has never happened before. I bought each of them a nail salon package for a manicure and pedicure, which I hope they all decide to go together this upcoming week. I am up before anyone else today, so I thought this would be a good opportunity to get some writing done. Today, the plan is to work around the house, getting a lot of small projects done that we have wanted to do for a while now. The women are going to work outside, planting flowers and such, while the men will be inside, doing some touch-up painting and replacing a toilet in the master bathroom. Exciting Mother's Day, right? No worries, the men will prepare a big feast later in the day for all to enjoy. We still need to go to the local grocery store, but I'm thinking of chicken on the grill, corn on the cob, mac and cheese, salad, rolls, and some kind of amazing dessert to be announced.

If there is any good news, states including South Carolina are starting to partially open up their businesses. COVID-19 is definitely not a thing of the past, but states are starting SLOWLY to let businesses open for customers. However, there are still restrictions, such as having to wear a mask at all times while in the store, and restaurants are only open to a 50 percent capacity, still remembering to social-distance. Forty-seven states are loosening their stay-at-home order restrictions this weekend.

Watching television this morning, I have some numbers regarding the coronavirus that are staggering. Around 1.2 million people in the United States have contacted the coronavirus. In just the month of April, 20.5 million jobs have been lost. Schools have closed through the end of the academic year in 48 states. Sadly, 77,744 people have perished from the virus.

Hopefully, these government officials know what they are doing opening back up businesses, beaches, restaurants, etc. Many workers going back to work are very nervous about the unknown and have a lot of questions for their bosses. I would want to know what my employer has done to make sure I was going to be safe, and having a "team meeting" before the workplace opened back up would be extremely wise for all parties involved. I can't imagine this isn't being done in all communities, but that is why the unknown is so scary. Tomorrow I go to my first GA meeting. Stay tuned!

Chapter 31

Hello, My Name Is . . .

Sunday, May 17

It has been a little over two weeks since I was arrested, and I can't honestly say each day gets a little better. One would think that the initial shock would have decreased, but I am here to say that would not be the case.

My sister flew back to Colorado yesterday, and my parents left earlier this morning. Having them all here was very therapeutic, and their unconditional love and support meant the world to me. Jenny has been VERY quiet all day, and I still worry about her more than I worry about myself. I will most likely just leave her alone today to unwind since all her in-laws just left. She is probably enjoying her quiet time and not having to worry about entertaining guests. She always wants to make everything perfect for everybody when they visit, and she usually does. A+ for hospitality goals to the teacher, Mrs. Bagwell . . . Honor roll!

I went to two GA meetings or sessions this week, Monday and Thursday nights, for an hour and fifteen minutes each. I really didn't know what to expect since this was a first for me. There were eight people there on Monday and nine people on Thursday, all with the same problem that I have—or should I say had. You come into these meetings, or at least I did, thinking the other addicts would be strange, weird, or odd. I feel awful that I judged individuals before meeting them. Sure enough, they weren't any different than me in most ways.

The first question you might have for me is, do you have

to say your name in front of the group and admit you have a problem. The answer to that is yes. Both sessions were conducted approximately the same way. The nights started off with introductions, counselor-led therapy that involved setting goals and being truthful to yourself first, and finishing off listening to each other's stories. I will have to say it helps seeing and hearing others struggle with their gambling addictions and the helplessness they feel at times.

At the last session, we had seven males and two females, who consisted of a doctor, daycare provider, architect, telemarketer, two construction workers, toll booth operator, housewife, and yours truly—definitely a variety of people who shared one common shortcoming, gambling. Even though all of the stories were similar in what we were going through, individually, the stories of how we ended up where we were at were totally different. The struggle is real! I looked in my Bible for a verse that discussed the phrase "life struggles." One of the better verses I discovered was from the book of Ephesians, chapter 3, verse 17. "Christ will make His home in your heart as your trust in Him. Your roots will grow down into God's love and keep you strong." I am planning on sharing this verse with the rest of the group at our next GA meeting. We are asked to bring a positive thought to each meeting and hopefully share it with the others if we feel inclined. Jenny just walked in and asked if I would stop writing because she wants to talk to me before we go to bed. Maybe she wants to go to my next GA meeting with me? Who knows!

Chapter 32

It's Over

Monday, May 18

It is 12:41 AM, and I haven't been to sleep yet. I haven't even lain down on my bed to try to go to sleep. The last journal entry I wrote was just slightly over three hours ago, and I am writing again, which is highly unusual. You might be thinking I am anxious about an upcoming hearing at the courthouse or nervous about my next meeting with my lawyer, where I need to start making some decisions about my future. Well, you are way off! You might be thinking that I regressed and started gambling again. Thankfully, that has not happened. It's worse if that is possible. By the way, it is possible! Jenny dropped another bombshell on me, letting me know that this is too much for her. She is going to file for divorce. The dreaded D-word hurt more than a Ronda Rousey armbar in one of her championship matches.

I sat there speechless for once in my life and truly did not know what to say. Obviously, she had given it A LOT of thought and decided she just couldn't do it—or did not want to try to go through the unknown. My soul mate, who I love more than life itself, just told me, "It's over!" The first thing that ran through my head was to give her a long hug and cry it out, but I was frozen on the couch and did absolutely nothing. I am not sure which was worse, getting arrested or having Jenny tell me she wants to separate. The way I am feeling now, the answer would definitely be the latter. Tears keep falling from my cheeks onto this paper, almost smearing the words. A small lake has formed on my desk near the paper.

I reluctantly agreed to find an apartment that I could move into until I found out what my criminal punishment would be. MJ and Chloe . . . (ten minutes passed). Sorry, I just can't put into words the pain! Excruciating! I am as low as a human can get at this second. If I could go outside and get struck by a bolt of lightning, I would, without hesitation, if I knew it would definitely happen. I need to pray now, over and over. I need His ears to hear me ask Him about what my purpose in life is and how I can serve Him until the day I am with Him. I am at the point where I need to surrender all to Him and praise Him for sticking with me through all my trials and tribulations.

Just yesterday, for some reason, call it curiosity, I looked online at my story that was all over the news and in the papers. Some of the comments from people that don't even know me were full of hate and extremely over-the-top vindictive. Yes, there were even a handful of death threats toward me. People who jump to conclusions and believe every word they read and then comment on the story without knowing both sides hold a special place in my heart. Pure ignorance! It is, unfortunately, the world we live in currently. This is where I need His strength to overcome when I feel overwhelmed. Don't even get me started about my Facebook page. I have gone from over 1,000 friends on the app to now under 700 in just a little over a week. Some of the messages in my inbox were not good and very spiteful. It does not take much in your life to go from being an A+ to an F in people's eyes. If you could pray for all my family and friends, Jenny and our kids especially, I would appreciate it very much. I would like to say I am going to go to the couch and try to get some sleep, but it is not going to happen—probably just look through the family photo albums.

Chapter 33

My New Pad

Monday, May 25

Moving from a 3,500-square-foot house into an 880-square-foot apartment was a culture shock this week. One week has passed since I wrote last, and I can say that I am totally moved. The apartment came furnished, which helped a lot with the move. Bringing over many boxes of my belongings was back-breaking since I live on the second floor. Unfortunately, my apartment does not have an elevator, so my hamstrings and lower back are a little sore. Okay, very sore!

My new place—or as the kids call it, my new pad—is located on a golf course and has a pool. It isn't like I am living in a shack. I wanted MJ and Chloe to feel safe and secure when they came over to stay with me on the weekends. Today is Memorial Day, so Jenny agreed to let them stay for half of the day. The kids and I decided to redecorate their bedroom they share, wash the car, and get a pizza. Little things like this are how I make it through each day. The kids seem to be handling the move as best as they can, but I know deep down they are hurting. As of this writing, Jenny and I are not talking, which has been extremely hard for me.

As I sit here nightly without my wife and kids, I feel a sense of loneliness that is unbearable. This is so new and fresh that I am not used to the silence. I can tell you I loathe it with every fiber in my body. I cannot stop crying when I am by myself, so I have to find ways to keep busy throughout the day.

Lying on the couch, staring intently at the television, flipping channels back and forth, my mind is elsewhere. I feel like I have attention deficit disorder (ADD) because I cannot concentrate at all, no matter how hard I try. My best guess is that at my school (or what used to be my school), 20 percent of the students are diagnosed with ADD or ADHD, with the H representing hyperactivity. Now, I understand much better how hard it is for these kids to try to function on a daily basis, and I have a new appreciation for each and every one of them.

I have a meeting with my lawyer tomorrow, and I am 99 percent sure as I sit here that I am going to tell him that I want to plead guilty and not go through the trial. I am so emotional that I do not want to hear all the bad news from the prosecutor in a multi-day trial. It would not be healthy for my loved ones nor for me. There can be a quick hearing that hopefully the judge will give me a break and take my past into consideration. A plea deal has to be the way to go, but the question is what the prosecutor will offer me that will be fair. Will my lawyer advise me to take the plea bargain? There are so many questions that need to be answered because I am having a hard time being patient. The inevitable is going to happen! Just how bad can it get! I need Jenny to make it through this, but where is she? Where is she? I am sooooo sorry, babe! My head hurts, my hand is shaking, and I can't function whatsoever. Please, Lord, help me! The struggle is all too real!

Chapter 34

Plea Bargain

Tuesday, May 26

It has been long, agonizing twenty-five days since my arrest. I have learned a lot about myself, good and bad. Today was a good day for me, which is actually saying a whole bunch. I am almost saying this sarcastically because my days lately stink, but I was able to get some relief today. Turning into a worrywart like my wife, Jenny, has been absolute madness. My personality has always been laidback and reserved, so this tumultuous event in my life has definitely changed me. And I don't like it! So I decided to ease my pain.

This morning at my lawyer's office, I indeed pulled the trigger and told him that I did not want to take this to a trial. I was willing to make a deal with the prosecutor if he would be fair regarding the punishment mentioned previously. My lawyer was a little concerned because he doesn't believe I can avoid jail time, plea bargain or not. I appreciate his honesty, but boy does it sting listening to his answers and advice. Knowing I have no past criminal history will help my case, as well as getting help with my problem by attending GA meetings. Bart, my lawyer, is just concerned with the amount of money I took (embezzled), the length of time I have been "borrowing" the money (ten years), and I didn't really show remorse for my actions in my meeting with Detective Jackson regarding my crimes. Lack of remorse? Really? I couldn't be more remorseful for my actions. Was I making excuses and not trying to tell the whole truth at that time? YES! But that doesn't mean that I'm not remorseful! Don't spin the truth!

I'm hoping for probation and a fine as my punishment with NO jail time. What good would it do for me to go sit in jail, wasting my time each day sitting there staring at a wall? Doing a thousand hours of community service would be more beneficial, in my opinion. Too bad, my opinion means absolutely nothing. The hearing I had in front of the magistrate judge two weeks ago took literally ten minutes. That is why I haven't even mentioned it yet. I plead not guilty at that time on the advice from my lawyer, Bart. Everything my lawyer tried, including bond reduction, was denied by the judge. It seemed like, whatever we were asking for, he was going to deny it without a second thought—no consideration whatsoever! My opinion (rights) did NOT matter! I am learning a lot about the judicial system and about myself. Regarding the judicial system, I am not a fan. That is the nicest and most Christian thing I can say.

The next question I have is, how long will it be for my next hearing if I do indeed take the plea bargain? COVID-19 has pushed back many trials. I'm hoping, since my case will only be a hearing, that it will be moved to the front of the list. One can dream! Bart said, in his opinion, it could happen depending on which judge I am assigned to for my hearing. There are three different judges for my county. Bart was hoping for Judge Campbell, who he thinks would be willing to not be as strict as his other two peers. Listening to the magistrate judge in my initial hearing, I was not impressed. Thankfully, he won't be present for my final hearing! Deny! Deny! Deny! Fair? No! NOT AT ALL! I am not a criminal. I lost my way, no excuses! Lord, help me find my way to you.

Chapter 35

Tough Decision

Friday, May 29

Trying to come to grips that I broke the law DOES make me a criminal, even though it is still hard to think, say, or admit it. Losing my wife, children, full-time job, career, house, insurance, and integrity is a bitter pill to swallow. I don't know how some people that are called career criminals function daily. Mentally, I am a walking zombie throughout each day. My secret has been eating at me for quite a while now. The angst of not seeing the kids—WOW! I can't tell you the pain will ever go away. Jenny, I miss you and love you! In the meantime . . .

The day came much earlier than expected. The prosecutor sent a report to my lawyer about the initial findings in my case. Included in the report was a plea bargain if I was interested. Bart called and told me to come to his office at the end of the day at 4:30 PM to discuss the report. The day seemed to drag, and it was difficult waiting the entire day, thinking negative thoughts. Reading a report about yourself in a negative light is a hard thing for anybody. I said a prayer before going to the meeting and went for a long walk at the beach to clear my head.

Bart started slowly looking over the discovery paper since he hadn't had too much time to thoroughly look it over. He apologized, saying it was his intent to skim through it at lunchtime, but his schedule was so packed with clients all day. It just didn't happen. Looking at it together and reading what was written was eye-opening.

Bart did a thorough job explaining all the legal terms in a language that I would comprehend. This was much appreciated! All that I asked of him was to be as straightforward as possible and not to leave any stone unturned. From the beginning, I have told him that this is my life and, after his legal advice, ultimately, the decision of what I want to do regarding the plea is mine. Boy, it truly was a tough decision after listening to Bart.

The state offered me this deal: one felony charge that would carry up to a ten-year sentence while the other three felony charges for embezzlement and fraud would be dropped and also a $25,000 fine. Hmm . . . up to a ten-year sentence? It could be less depending on the judge. Anything over a year would be served in a maximum-security prison, not at the jail. Bart did mention that if it was anywhere from one to five years, the prison I would go to would be a level 1 facility. Meaning, I would have more freedoms than a level 2 through level 5, where I would hardly have any freedoms. Freedoms or luxuries to me mean I wouldn't have to be locked down as much in my cell. I have heard that in some prisons, you are locked in your cell for up to twenty-three hours each day. I can't even fathom this! How do you rehabilitate somebody who can't come out of his cell ALL day? Do I take this plea or not? My lawyer said, in his opinion, he would say yes. He can work it out to get us a hearing next month, saying we can get this done and be in/out of the courthouse within thirty to forty-five minutes. Of course, my out would be in handcuffs heading to the local jail, awaiting transport to wherever they want to send me. I told Bart that I would take the weekend and think it over. I will call him on Monday with my decision. What would you do?

Chapter 36

Deep Breath

Sunday, May 31

Having MJ and Chloe all day yesterday and all day today was extra special for me. I am thankful for their unconditional love and the special bond that we have together. I have already recently caused them some heartache. Oh, if I could only turn the clock back. Unfortunately, I know more is coming. They don't know this yet, and I need to figure out how I am going to tell them. Lord, protect their hearts.

When it comes right down to it, I want nothing to do with a trial knowing full well that I broke the law. The media presence would be intense, and that is not fair to my family. My decision as of 10:34 PM, Sunday, May 31, is to accept the plea deal from the prosecutor and the state of South Carolina. I will beg for mercy in front of the judge, banking on the fact that he or she will be lenient due to my lack of criminal history. I'm fairly certain I can serve a couple of years in prison without going off the deep end. I need to take the yucky medicine even though I don't want to. Once again, I brought this upon myself, and I agree I deserve to be punished. BUT . . . my sentence should be light! Fair! JUST! I have prayed about this a few times tonight. As long as I don't chicken out by tomorrow morning when I call my attorney to give him the news, I am finally at peace with my decision. All I have to do is take a deep breath and let him know what I decided. No going back! Man up to my mistake! What the heart thinks the mouth speaks. I learned this from my grandma years ago, and it has stuck with me all these years.

I want to call Jenny and get her advice, but that would be in vain since she is not talking to me. When a person loves somebody that much and all forms of communication stop, it cuts deep. Everybody reacts differently—I get it. Boy, do I get it! Going down the wrong road, now I finally admit that I messed up. It almost seems like no matter what I do or say, it won't matter. Sad but true! I will NEVER totally get over how much pain I caused or my internal pain. But I will give Jenny time to deal with her pain, confusion, and anger. Hopefully, it will be months, not years, for her to forgive me, and I didn't intentionally try to hurt her or anyone. I'm sorry, I'm sorry, I'm sorry!

My gut feeling is that I won't write for a while since I have been writing quite a bit lately. My journal entries are not meant to be sad or depressing, but I feel like I want to give you the most realistic picture I can of what my family and I are going through the closer we get to the decision. Imagine having your face plastered on the TV, newspaper, and on social media, telling people that you are a thief and a criminal. Seriously, think about this! Prayer, deep breaths, long hot showers, writing, and my family by my side supporting me are how I can hold my head up high, knowing who I truly am. I pray and understand He has no limit and is calling us to a holy life. He stands by me and gives me strength each morning to make it through the day seven times a week. Praise Him!

Chapter 37

Time Is Ticking

Sunday, June 21

Three weeks have passed since I have last written. Today has been special for two reasons. One, today is Father's Day. I spend the day not only with MJ and Chloe but also with my father, who is in town visiting with my mother. Having five people stuffed into a small two-bedroom apartment brings things into perspective, making me long for my house that was rather large. Doesn't really matter, to be honest. The more, the merrier. It is good medicine for me to hear the chatter and laughter at a time that I definitely need it. It is also my father's eightieth birthday today.

Get to the point already, you might be thinking. It has been three weeks, so please fill me in on what has been happening. I have had four different appointments with Bart, my lawyer, in the last twenty-one days. Did I chicken out on agreeing to the plea deal? No, most certainly not! Bart said he would work with the prosecutor the best he could before taking everything to the judge. I appreciated his hard work, and now all I could do was trust him.

This is what I did just three days ago when I had my final hearing before I came before the judge for his decision. I plead guilty in the hearing this Thursday afternoon with my parents in attendance for support. He set a date for what punishments would be levied against me for Wednesday, July 1, at 1:00 PM. This is the day when, if I am serving time in the Department of Corrections

(DOC), I would be led out of the courthouse in handcuffs in front of the local media.

You would think that would not bother me anymore, but it definitely does not get any easier. Get this! At the final hearing on Thursday, the prosecutor asked the judge, since I have now pleaded guilty, that I should immediately be placed into custody awaiting the decision on July 1. Bart, who was angered and perplexed by this announcement, was adamant that I still remain out until this date. I posted bond, followed all rules since posting bond, and I am not a threat or danger to society. The judge ruled in my favor, agreeing with Bart that I have upheld my part of the bargain since my arrest. Time is ticking now with the countdown to July 1. My heart almost stopped ticking when the prosecutor pleaded to the judge to put me in jail right now. Bart had not even said this could be a possibility, so that caught me off guard for sure. The judge finally ruled something in my favor . . . thankfully! The judge!

From what I have heard, Judge Murphy is nicknamed Maximum Murphy. This made me feel really good . . . NOT! When he was in his first term, his sentences were lengthy, and he was known as a no-nonsense type. My initial reaction when I first saw him was he didn't smile much or at all. His body language portrayed somebody who you didn't mess with ever. Maybe this is the way all judges are. I have never stepped inside of a courtroom my entire life. Fifty years old, and I have never served on a jury. I have only received one letter saying that I have been selected to be on a jury. When I called the night before, the automated voice said the trial had been canceled and not to report. I do not want to have any preconceived notions about Judge Murphy, so everything I have heard I am taking with a grain of salt. All cases are different. Hopefully, he can realize how the media has portrayed me is not who I am. Has he seen me on the television? I would assume yes. Will he give me a harsh sentence to make an example out of me? He is a public servant who will want to be re-elected by the citizens of his county. That is a lot of pressure for him to not let me off the hook. The media might make him look bad since they have tried to portray me as a loathsome individual. The more I think about this, the more stressed I get.

Jenny agreed to meet with me on the last day of June to discuss our future. Knowing when we meet, she is due to deliver baby Jacob in two short weeks is a concern . . . huge concern! She texted me and asked if we could meet for an hour to clear the air. She also mentioned that she sat down with MJ and Chloe and let them know what might happen. When I texted back to ask about their reaction, I only received an emoji with a crooked frown. Our discussion needs to happen, but at this point, I am beyond words. Saying I'm sorry again won't mean anything. Until she is willing to forgive me, we are at a stalemate. Hopefully, she realizes that the Lord watches over her, and in her distress, her cries will be heard. We have drifted away from the Lord in recent years; my hope is we reach out to God for peace, happiness, and contentment. It is a weird feeling to know we will see each other and not know if I can hug her. Will she let me? Can you say awkward? Of course, I want to hug her and not let go. Will I shed tears? Yes, most likely. Will I sob like a hungry baby with a soiled diaper? Maybe. Tick . . . Tick . . . Tick . . .

Chapter 38

I Will Be Back

Tuesday, June 30

Tomorrow is the day! I can't say I'm looking forward to it, yet at the same time, I am ready to have all this behind me. I feel like I have aged ten years in the last year, and that is no joke. MJ and Chloe helped me move some of my belongings back to the house. It is a kick in the pants to see all you have left is packed in boxes stored in your garage. Not the best feeling in the world. Luckily, Jenny agreed to let me store these items for the time being.

My meeting with Jenny today (or as I call it, our "get-together") was tear-jerking and difficult. Trying to put it into words is hard for me to do. Writing comes so easily for me, but in this instance, I am unsure of how to put those words on paper to accurately fill you in on what was said. We have two amazing children, with one more on the way. I am proud to say that we raised them the right way. I love her still, and I always will to the end. Regrets? Most definitely! I could go on and on, but I won't. I can't. It hurts too badly! Enough said! I wish I could tell you of a happy ending. I can't. Not yet.

Also, I had an impromptu meeting with my lawyer, Bart, late this afternoon. He talked with the prosecutor this morning, and both agreed to a deal that they wanted to present to the judge tomorrow. I didn't even know this was possible, but I guess it saves time as long as the judge agrees that the sentence is fair for all parties involved. Bart shared with me that my sentence would include incarceration of four years, having to serve three-fourths of that time in a low-level maximum-security prison. The fine of $25,000 and two years' probation would be part of the deal as well. Bart advised me to take the deal, and he was 99.9 percent sure Judge Murphy would agree to it.

I let it sink in for a bit before I did indeed say yes to the deal. There was no reason to drag it on any further. However, I had hoped for no time behind bars; deep down, I knew it had to be. I will do my best to stay positive and be a mentor for the other inmates who are still searching for who they are and who they want to be. God has been there for me, and I know He will be with me every step of the way the next few years and beyond.

As I sit here tonight, I can tell you one thing for certain—my life is not over. I will be back, striving to be better than ever. Part I of my life was memorable for many reasons. Part II is a chance for me to make a difference in a way that I might now even realize yet. That is something I can really look forward to. God has a plan for me, and I can't wait to see what it is. Happy ending now? Maybe.

To my family, thank you for everything! My childhood was fantastic, thanks to my parents and sister. MJ and Chloe, you two are perfect and don't ever change. Jenny, twenty amazing, memorable years—I hope you find peace and move on to bigger and better things. Change the world!

Chapter 39

Until Next Time

Thursday, July 2

This might be a little bit of a surprise that I am able to update you on my status after court yesterday. I borrowed some paper and a pencil from another inmate. One day later, here are some of my thoughts on what has happened in the past twenty-four hours. My lawyer, Bart, was able to visit me earlier today just like he promised to check up on me.

Yesterday, what else can I say besides the day was awful! My emotions were under control the entire time in and outside the courtroom. Yes, there were a plethora of members from the press with cameras following my every step and movement. It is extremely difficult to keep your composure and not say something negative in their direction. Understanding they are there to do their job does not make it any easier to stay quiet. I wanted to shout, "Go film somebody doing something positive instead of following little old me walking through the courthouse!" Would you like to make a comment, Mr. Bagwell? This is something that is going through my head over and over again last night and all day today.

I have been told by the other inmates that I will most likely be held here at the county jail for approximately two weeks before I am transferred to the Department of Corrections Regional Facility. When I arrived here last night, eventually, I ended up in BLOCK E, along with twenty-three other inmates who were already here waiting for their release or to be transferred to prison like me.

There are twelve cells with two inmates residing in each cell. I was told to take my belongings to cell number 7, and I would be on the top bunk. Bunk beds? I haven't ever slept on a bed bunk. Getting up and down has been a challenge.

My Bunkie, as you call the guy you share a cell with, is much younger than me. His name is Matt, and he is also awaiting transfer to the regional facility. He let me know he knew who I was already, which was odd. I assumed he was a former student at my school or had a sibling attend there recently. Nope, not the case. He said that the entire cell block saw my story on the local news last night. I was the lead story on the local evening news. Wow, how humiliating! All I could think was I hope that MJ and Chloe weren't watching their father being negatively portrayed.

One last thing that you might find of interest is that, because of the COVID-19 virus, all inmates must wear a mask at all times. The only time we are not required to wear our masks is when we sleep, eat, or shower. The officials and inmates take this virus seriously, which is nice to see. Definitely coming here, I was uneasy about what to expect being housed with a large group of people and not wanting to catch this contagious, deadly disease. I still pray daily for the research doctors to find a vaccine ASAP to stop the spread of this incredibly dangerous virus.

I would like to end this chapter of my life with what else than a top ten list and a positive quote. I wish you well, and you never know, maybe you will hear from me again. Hmmmm . . .

Top ten things I miss already besides my family:

1. My iPhone—I feel lost without it.
2. DQ Chocolate Chip Cookie Dough Blizzard—my weakness.
3. Pillow—yep, no pillows are given out in jails.
4. Beach—loved going on long walks on the boardwalk.
5. Deep dish pizza—every Friday night, not this Friday or for a while.
6. Nike running shoes—my feet may never recover.
7. Clock—you never know what time it is in here.
8. Jenny's home-cooked meals—chicken enchiladas were my favorite dish.
9. Electric toothbrush—the one I just received, yikes! Not electric!

10. Pets—there is nothing better than walking the dog through the neighborhood.

Quote of the day: motto from my school, Westmoreland Learning Academy:

"Be safe, be responsible, and be respectable."
God bless, Nyles Bagwell.

Part II LCI

Chapter 40

The New Normal

If you are wondering what LCI stands for, you are probably not alone. I was thinking the same thing when I first heard these initials. LCI stands for Livesay Correctional Institution and is located in Spartanburg, South Carolina. It is a level 1 facility that houses inmates that are nonviolent offenders, rehabilitating them before they get released. Unfortunately, I am one of those inmates residing in this facility. After spending several days in the county jail, I was transported here three weeks later, presumably for the duration of my sentence imposed by the judge.

My brain is telling me not to write this part of my life story as daily journal entries but just day-by-day observations. It is called free writing. I will write about whatever comes to my mind. My first impression of this facility was favorable, if that was even possible. Maybe it was just because it was definitely an upgrade from the cramped, unkempt county jail. This place feels like a country club compared to the jail. Don't get me wrong, though— living here is definitely going to be a challenge. I would say more mentally than physically. However, being fifty years old, I am feeling some minor aches and pains already. Who wouldn't when you go from sleeping on a comfortable king mattress to a thin foam mat with no pillow?

Let me backtrack a little going back a few weeks to the day I left the jail. Leaving by van, nine other inmates and I were brought to a place where it will be hard for me to think of one positive thing to say about it. To be factual and to even write this, I am somewhat embarrassed. We were taken to a diagnostic center to be processed and later placed in a facility that would fit our needs for our best rehabilitation. The part I am embarrassed by was that I didn't even know what city this facility was in when we arrived. I assumed that I was going to prison to serve my sentence, but I awkwardly found out that was not the case.

Prisoner, inmate, convict—pick one that you want to call me. I will, for now, call myself an inmate. It doesn't sound as bad as the other two, in my opinion. Anyway, inmates are brought to this regional diagnostic center first. This facility is considered a level 5, which would be the highest level with hardly any freedoms. This meant we were in our cells twenty-three hours a day, seven days a week. We were let out for meals from 7:00 AM to 7:25 AM and 4:00 PM to 4:25 PM. Usually, around 10:00 PM, we were allowed to take a ten-minute scorching-hot or ice-cold shower. I am not exaggerating at all when trying to describe the water temperature of the showers. Showers A and C were so hot that you couldn't even stand underneath the showerhead. Meanwhile, showers B and D were the exact opposite, with the water being colder than you could imagine. I called taking showers at night "bird baths" because I would just splash water on me to wet myself down to the best of my ability. The towels we were given were just a bit bigger than the size of a washcloth (not kidding) and smelled like my son MJ's dirty socks. That is when I knew that this "challenge" would be taxing. It is hard to stay positive when you sit in your cell ALL day and can't even get a good shower. Come on!

When I say sit in the cell all day, I want to be more specific in my description. When you arrive, you are given a brown sack with a few necessities, such as hygiene items. In addition, you receive a mat, sheet, and blanket. The discolored, outdated sheet is about two-thirds the size of your mat. I felt like a lost child at the mall, looking around without a clue in the world on how to solve problems in a new environment. Luckily, I had a bunkie who was helpful and showed me a few things that would help me in the beginning and down the road.

As I stretched out on my new (or should I say old) mat and looked up, thinking what to do next, I realized instantaneously that this is it. Just lie here and do nothing. No paper or pencils to write letters, no book to read, no television to watch, no playing cards, no ANYTHING. You are allowed to order items from the

store if you have money, but it would take at least one week.
An order just went in right before I arrived. This meant I could
not order until next week AND had to wait another week for
the order to show up on our range—two weeks of maddening
boredom. Fortunately, my bunkie let me borrow the book he had
just finished up. It was missing pages, though, so some parts of
the story did not make sense, but it was better than nothing. It
was a romance novel, and for the life of me, I can't remember the
name of it. It was the first romance novel that I have ever read,
and it will be the last. Not a fan! It wasn't at all believable!

My Bunkie, who had already been here for almost three
weeks, was due to leave any day. He slept a lot. Who wouldn't?
When he was awake, the best way to describe him was that he
liked to tell stories. I would call his stories more like tall tales. As
you know (or maybe you don't know), I like to share stories about
myself too. My stories are entertaining and factual. His stories
were entertaining and fictional. At least it gave me something
to do. One of my better life skills is that I am a good listener.
Being a principal for almost twenty years helped me to become a
better listener. Not sure if my wife, Jenny, would agree with this
statement. She mentioned more than once that I have selective
hearing. I think some wives say this about their husbands, though.
My wife is no exception.

Since I like to share funny stories, how about I do my best
to tell you a story that my bunkie told me? There are five to ten
"doozies" that he shared with me; it is hard to pick just one. How
about this one, for starters?

A little background information about my bunkie might be
a good start. He was homeless and lived in a tent downtown near
several other people who had run into their share of bad luck.
He was employed at a factory that manufactured a product that
was to be shipped out and distributed to many stores in different
communities. He did not tell me what the product was, only that
it was his job to package it to be shipped. He mentioned that the
money he made he spent on drugs, and he was an addict for the
past eight years.

One day, while sleeping in his tent, he awoke to the smell of
bacon cooking. Who doesn't? A large group of people was making
breakfast in the parking lot across from where he lived. Feeling

hungry and almost as the smell of bacon lured him over there to check out the scene, he had hoped the group might possibly share some with him. Indeed, they did share some with him. According to him, the group was a bunch of guys and gals that were riding cross-country on their motorcycles. Striking up a conversation with one of the bikers, he inquired if there was any extra, he would love to reap the benefits of anything they were willing to give. To his delight, he ate a meal fit for a king. French toast, biscuits and gravy, scrambled eggs, pancakes, coffee cake, and fresh-squeezed orange juice, just to list a few things he ate or drank.

I, only half believing him, questioned how in the world you could eat all of that in one sitting. I almost felt bad about questioning whether or not he was telling the truth. Not sure why I didn't believe him. He just seemed like he was adding on to the story to make it livelier. After what I have been through lately, I did not want to judge somebody without getting to know the whole story.

The end of the story is why I am sharing this with you. He said that the gentleman who gave him all that food also gave him his motorcycle jacket. That made me pause because I would assume somebody part of a motorcycle club would never give his jacket away, especially to somebody he had just met. The story gets even better. My bunkie excitedly whispered that after he got the guy's jacket, the guy gave him a manila envelope that was passed around to the different club members. Inside the envelope was more than $1,000, all for him.

Now, remember, I used to be a principal, and I have heard a lot of different made-up stories, excuses, and lies to last me a lifetime. My bunkie's story had a lot of holes in it, and I applaud his effort on keeping a straight face the whole time he told me the story. Does anybody reading this believe his story to be true? Every two or three hours between my naps and mealtimes, he told me a different story about his experiences living as a homeless man. Each story was a little more suspicious than the one before. But you know what? Listening to his stories kept my mind off my problems, which helped reduce my stress level. Try lying on a mat all day in a room the size of a bathroom with a person you just met and not feel sorry for yourself. Your mind wanders and keeps coming back to all the people you hurt because of your addiction.

Praying was a lifesaver, but I want to be completely honest with you. I am human, and prayer helped, but it wasn't enough. I needed more help, but what could that be? Your emotions go from loneliness to frustration to anger and usually always comes back to loneliness. I miss my wife and kids! You might be thinking I can call them every once in a while. Absolutely not! While you are housed at this diagnostic center, there are no incoming or outgoing phone calls. Brutal!

I would be remiss if I didn't mention that my wife was due to give birth to our third child while here. Having no communication with the outside world, I was not aware if baby Jacob had been born until I finally received a letter in the mail from my parents telling me I was a proud father of a baby boy. I felt a sense of relief like no other, but I also felt like a loser for not being able to be there for my son's birth and to support my wife. I remember lying there on my mat that night and every night after, crying myself to sleep from anxiety and depression. Why me?

After a week, my first bunkie left to be transported to his next facility. I learned that when you are told you are leaving, the correctional officers do not tell you what prison you are going to until you are in handcuffs. Guess they have had issues in the past with inmates throwing a fit and refusing to go because they did not want to go to a certain prison for one reason or another.

My second bunkie arrived seven hours after my first bunkie left. In and out . . . in and out . . . didn't take long! My new bunkie was a good ol' boy from the south who came to the diagnostic center because of armed robbery and drug possession. That is another thing I discovered while I was there. They did not put inmates together who had the same charges that they were found guilty of from the state of South Carolina. I'm sure there were some cells where both inmates had similar charges, but all the inmates on my range had different charges. I had the feeling that everybody would be complaining about the judicial system and saying that they were innocent. To my surprise, I did not really hear anybody say this. Some were unhappy with how long their sentence was, and come to think of it, most of the inmates around me were appealing their judge's decision because of the length of their sentence. I felt like I was the only one who did not appeal the judge's decision. Most of the inmates around me had lengthy sentences, ranging anywhere from twelve to sixty years. I almost felt bad saying that I had a shorter sentence, so I decided not to talk about my case too much. Probably the smartest decision I made while I was there. The more I thought about it, the more depressed I would become. My second bunkie's best quality was that he was quiet, and he slept a lot, which was actually kind of to my liking.

As an added bonus and out of the blue, the facility added a movie time you could go to from either 7:00–9:00 PM or 9:30–11:30 PM every night. I chose to usually go to the later movie, which meant that shower time for that group did not start until after midnight. Getting out of the cell for an extra two hours every night was huge. Little things like this mean a lot, and fortunately, the movie was just one added extra bonus. A church service on Sunday night was also offered to all of the inmates from 5:00 PM to 6:00 PM. Another hour out of my cell—jackpot! Church, amen! We sang two songs, and the sound of music has never sounded better. It actually cheered me up for a short time. The pastor's message was about humility and forgiveness of sin, and it couldn't have come at a better time. Remember earlier when I said how big of a challenge it is to stay positive in this place? Game on! Well, God heard me and sent me a pastor and some movies. How about that? Maybe I can wish for an early release, so I can be free. LOL.

I met with a counselor who discussed my immediate future. He was helpful but not at all friendly. Smiles go a long way, and I can truthfully say he did not smile once in our fifteen-minute conference. He mentioned in the next day or two that I would be leaving the diagnostic center and heading to a different facility that I most likely would be at for my entire sentence. Gulp! New place, new people. I just started to get used to this place. However, I am leaving a level 5 facility and going to a level 1 facility, which is a major upgrade. This brought a gigantic smile to my face. An actual smile!

Chapter 41

Welcome to Your New Home

Now, I sit here today at LCI, knowing I have made it out of the county jail and the regional diagnostic center. I am moving to the next and possibly the last phase of my sentence. LCI is considered an open-door facility instead of the cells that I was previously stuck in. I can still hear the clanking of the door closing, knowing it would not open for several hours until the next meal. I have always been a person who doesn't sit well being locked up, and the transition has been harder than I thought. I think back to MJ and Chloe every once in a while, saying they were bored. Well, I am here to say that I now understand how they were feeling. Actually, times one hundred! Dad's boredom is greater than MJ/Chloe's boredom. I'm very competitive, and I hate to lose. This time, I wish I was on the losing end.

Just arriving in a new facility, I met my counselor for the first time. She looks to be approximately thirty years old with long, curly red hair. It is Friday, so the staff had a relaxed dress day. She wore blue jeans and a University of South Carolina black polo shirt. Get this! When she greeted me, she was smiling. Yes! Her name is Lucille Granderson, but she said to call her Lucy. She had my file open and wanted to discuss a plan of rehabilitation for me during my time here at LCI. Pretty standard, I guess. Having a job would be enjoyable to keep me busy throughout the day. Sitting around this past month has made me feel lazy and lethargic—not a good combination. She presented many different opportunities for employment, which was music to my ears. I was thinking about something in the education field, but my brain was telling me to go in a different direction. Try something new.

Employment within LCI ranged from working in the factory, cooking in the kitchen, outdoor landscape crew, maintenance, or shelving books in the library. I left one of the jobs out on purpose because it is the one I selected. Drumroll, please! I am the newly appointed clerk in the chaplain's office. Why not? I narrowed my list down to the kitchen and the chaplain's office—a tough choice, to be honest. I love to cook, but I knew deep down I would probably gain twenty to thirty pounds during my stay here. Nibbling and snacking would be my downfall. Working at the chapel, I felt I could continue my walk toward becoming a better Christian. I start next week, and I'm not really sure what my job entails yet—something to look forward to, that's for sure.

I turned in my phone to Lucy, which means I should be able to call family members and friends sometime in the next three to five days. I can't wait to hear my kids' voices! I have only talked to them once since I was escorted out of the courtroom on that dreadful July day. But it has been three and a half weeks since I have last communicated with them. I'm sure most of the conversation will revolve around their summer break and, of course, the arrival of their baby brother, Jacob. I was thinking last night while lying on my mat, not able to sleep, about not having to change any diapers this time around. Not that I changed a lot of MJ's and Chloe's diapers. Jenny probably changed 85–90 percent of the diapers of our two older kids. Looking back at it now, I would give anything to be there changing one of Jacob's diapers. I'm hoping, when I start talking to some of the other inmates, they have children that they are going to talk about. Right now, I have kept to myself mainly and only have had a brief dialogue with a few of the guys.

I started in the chaplain's office today as a clerk. It felt a little strange working again, but it made me feel like a man again for the first time in quite a while. Not working takes its toll on you as an individual. You get used to doing the same thing day in and day out, but when your schedule gets interrupted, you feel stressed. Getting up early and knowing you are going to work is a good feeling. Personally, I think my day went by much faster than a day I wasn't working. That's great news!

I worked side by side all day with another offender who

told me to call him Byrd. He is a six-foot-eight, 250-plus-pound African-American gentleman who is extremely friendly and easygoing. Although I am six years older than him, I feel so small and like a little kid when I am standing next to him. Thinking back, I don't think I have ever worked with somebody as tall as him. His size is kind of intimidating, but he was so positive and helpful that I know we would work really well together. He has three kids too. So, we have something in common, and he enjoys talking about them to boot. I did not share with him that I used to be a principal. Not sure why!

The first thing I saw when I walked in was a sign on the wall that read, "I believe in God even when He is silent, just like I believe in the sun even when it is not shining." For some reason, reading this brought a big smile to my face. Maybe the sign made me feel like I was in my office at school. Positive messages make me perk up, and I always try to relate them to something.

This sign made me think back to when I was really struggling, and I decided I needed our Lord Jesus Christ to help me through this low time in my life. I stayed away from Him for a while, but I knew I needed Him back for me to get through each day. Did He lead me to the chaplain's office for employment to be closer to Him? In my heart, I truly feel He did, or at least He gave me the wisdom and inspiration to go down this path. Mentoring people who are also struggling (and some have been struggling for years) is something that I should be very good at while I'm here. Hmmm . . . giving advice, being a good listener, setting goals for the future, and problem-solving—where have I used these life skills? Oh, that's right, when I was a principal! Including God in the conversation is just the cherry on top or the frosting on the cake. I have only been working for one day here, but this is the "it" factor. "It" is something I need so that I don't go CRAZY!

Chapter 42

Hello, Dad!

Today was the day! I finally got the chance to call MJ and Chloe this afternoon. I was hoping Jenny would be a part of the conversation, but it was not to be. By all means, it hurts, and my pain is overwhelming not communicating with her. The pain she is feeling might never go away, and I am trying to come to grips with this fact. I am on the fence about whether or not to write her a letter expressing my feelings. For now, I will bide my time and be patient. Talking to the kids brought two different emotions to the forefront. First was pure elation throughout the entire thirty-minute call. The other emotion would be a feeling of melancholy when I hung up, knowing I would not talk to them again until next week. Trying to stay upbeat!

Our conversation went really well. Their voices sounded strong, and there was no awkward silence during the call. Half of the conversation was about their little brother, Jacob. They both said he cries a lot. Thankfully, they didn't say Jenny was the one who was doing the crying. I asked if they have helped change any diapers yet. All I got back was no chance of that happening.

It is hard to sit here and listen to their voices and realize what I am missing back at home. Not being there for MJ and Chloe's sporting events, music or dance recitals, school functions, award ceremonies, and other important happenings is heartbreaking. How about Jacob's first word, step, tooth, and all the other firsts? Holiday? Ouch! I have thought and thought about these things a million times over.

Recently, I keep coming back to the idea that I can help

these younger offenders by stressing the word "family." They can go back in time and think of something or someone that had or made a positive influence in their lives, NO matter how bad of a childhood they had. Most guys in here have had awful upbringings, but there is ALWAYS an event or person in their life that they can look back on with fond memories. I'm thinking it is time for a top ten list looking back on my favorite childhood memories. Why not!

1. My pet beagle, Norton—I got this amazing, family-friendly dog when I was five years old.
2. Lakehouse—I grew up living at this house until I was twelve years old when we moved to the city.
3. Vacations—every summer for probably fifteen straight years, we would go on a two-week vacation traveling around the great USA.
4. Sports—my true love was baseball, and I can still remember hitting my first home run.
5. Church family—Sunday from 10:00 AM to 2:00 PM, we had two services and lunch in between. There were lots of great people and fun-filled activities.
6. Little general store—riding our bikes through the trails in the woods on a two- to three-mile path to buy candy, soda pop, or ice cream.
7. Lake—whether it was swimming, diving off the pier, fishing, or ice skating in the winter, there was always something to do.
8. Blizzard of '78—being stuck at home for a week and trying to tunnel our way out the front door was fascinating for a young kid like me.
9. Sister—the first time we stayed home without my parents, we got into a fight and gave each other a fat lip. I probably deserved it. ☐
10. 1984 Chicago Cubs team—they were one win away from going to the World Series but unfortunately choked against the San Diego Padres.

Do you know how hard that was to narrow it down to just ten things from your whole childhood? If I was still a betting man, I am pretty sure if I made this same list tomorrow, it would change when I thought back and remembered other cool times of my early years. My plan is to write the kids every week or two and share a top ten list with them. I am pretty sure it would bring a big smile to their faces, looking back in time about positive memories of our lives together or just mine. I have shared some of my childhood stories with them, but I think I am going to send them this list of my favorite childhood memories with more details added.

I have decided that writing and listening to music are my two favorite activities to do when I have free time each day. Both let me get away, and it is my time just to relax and think. Everybody is different. Most inmates here play cards, watch TV, or exercise in their free time. I do enjoy walking around the track if it is not too hot outside. The summertime in South Carolina gets pretty hot and humid. I repeat, hot and humid!

If I choose to stay in and not get any exercise, sometimes I get on my tablet that LCI gives each inmate at orientation. I had no idea I would receive a tablet upon arrival, and from what I have heard from the other inmates, the tablets are something they just started passing out six months before I arrived. I don't use the tablet too much, but it is nice to have when there is nothing else to do. Streaming music, movies, and TV programs are available for purchase on the tablet. I have already shared that I listen to music, so having access to this app has been a plus. Also, there are games on the tablet, e-books, the ability to order commissary items from the store, and an app to check messages. Looking at some of the items on the commissary app, I am dreaming of eating some actual "real food" for a change. Eventually, I will write about the difference between eating at the chow hall and eating food off our commissary list. Eye-opening!

What I really found cool is that when I call the kids, I can use my tablet to talk to them. There is a phone app on the tablet that I will use weekly to call the kids and rotate calling my parents, sister, aunts and uncles, and cousins, to name a few. There is not a camera on the tablet, so I will NOT be able to send pictures. However, in my message app, I am allowed to receive pictures and videos, which are a Godsend when I am feeling low.

Everything costs money on the tablet. Nothing is free. The inmates who choose not to work and don't have any help from family members on the outside are not able to do much of anything since everything costs money. That is why I am confused on why an inmate would not want to work. Just having a little spending money goes a long way.

Chapter 43

Time to Eat

Chow hall today was an experience. Let me be honest, I have always been a picky eater, so I don't like as many types of foods that other people do. Here was today's lunch menu: cheesy potato casserole, carrots, pinto beans, two slices of bread, and a piece of cake. Maybe some of you (or even the majority of you) are thinking, what is he complaining about? Nothing out of the ordinary, so what's his deal? Well, the cheesy potato casserole is not cheesy. The best adjective that describes this casserole would be watery. Every entrée and side has water added to stretch it further among the inmates. The carrots and beans are always undercooked, I'm told by the others, and today was no exception. The cake tasted like sawdust, and now I'm not a fan of cake. Literally, all I ate was the two pieces of bread, half the small piece of cake, and a cup of water. This is something I have to look forward to on a daily basis. Some of the inmates do not come to the chow hall. Instead, they stay back at their unit and cook something they bought off the commissary. Most food items that are bought off the commissary can be heated in the microwave or in a hot pot that you can purchase from the store. The inmates do not have access to a stove or oven.

I already placed my first order from the commissary, and I'm eagerly awaiting its arrival in the next few days. I am going to write two top ten lists regarding the food eaten here at LCI and, my guess, at most other prisons. I nonchalantly asked nearly twenty inmates about commissary food that is a must and chow hall foods that I should stay away from. I found it interesting that a lot of their answers were similar even though everybody has their own likes and dislikes. Of course, the menu is limited, as is the commissary store, for variety and selection. My positive attitude is telling me to start with the high-quality list of foods from the store. Let's go, or should I say, "Let's eat!"

1. Ramen noodle soup—it is easy to microwave with a variety of flavors, such as chili, Cajun chicken, and picante beef.
2. Iced honey buns—if you love sweets, which who doesn't, this is the number one sweet treat for inmates.
3. Meat logs—different varieties include hot-and-spicy sausage, beef salami, or beef summer sausage. They are a good complement for soups and rice.
4. Rice—I am thinking of the TV show *Survivor*, where the contestants live on rice. Guess what, so do inmates. Rice is a filler.
5. Tortilla shells—inmates use tortillas to make tacos, burritos, enchiladas, and cut strips to put into soups and for desserts.
6. Cheese bars—small bars of cheese are cut up and used in many different dishes. Favorites are jalapeno, provolone, mozzarella, and sharp cheddar.
7. Cans of soda pop—I am not a big soda drinker, but it has sugar, so I am pretty sure I will buy a six-pack every once in a while. Pepsi products are offered.
8. Cookies—there are so many different types, it will make your head spin. My favorites will be chocolate chip and peanut butter.
9. Chips—spicy and BBQ corn chips, tortilla and nacho chips, and a variety of potato chips are available. Corn chips are the best buy, according to inmate.com.
10. Coffee—this is probably number 1 or number 2 on the list. Since I don't drink coffee, I moved it to the bottom. Most inmates are addicted to coffee.

Since it seems like the chow hall does not put any spices or seasonings into any of the food, these items are popular to purchase as well. Salt-and-pepper shakers, garlic powder, minced onion, granulated sugar, and hot sauce are always good to have around. I guess I better start working overtime at work to afford all of these. I was hoping to drop twenty pounds while I am here, but eating honey buns and cookies and drinking soda won't help this wish of being skinny.

This list was created based on the fact that I have eaten in the chow hall for a week now and already know what I like and what I loathe. I know you might like some of the foods I list, but I'm telling you right now, prison food is NOTHING like what you have at home or in a restaurant. Trust me!

1. Pinto beans—they are undercooked, rock hard, and tasteless. Served daily.
2. Cabbage—it has a funny taste and an odd color.
3. Peas—I never have been a fan of peas. While I am here, I plan on not even attempting to eat even one.
4. Fish patty—some inmates actually like this lunch entrée, but not yours truly. It's processed, cold, and hard to digest.
5. Carrots—cooked, not raw. See above and re-read number 3 (peas), and it would apply to carrots. Not eating even one!
6. Chili—if my wife, Jenny, was cooking, I would eat two bowls. Here at LCI, I will pass every time. No spices, no seasonings, no thanks!
7. Vegetable soup—it looks like and tastes like it has been sitting in the kettle for at least one week.
8. Rotini—I have been here for about a week, and we have had rotini or something almost identical three times. Overkill!
9. Irish blend vegetables—yep, another vegetable makes it to the list. I'm dying for a piece of fruit. Somebody send me an orange, please!
10. Pancakes—I absolutely love pancakes at home! What we have here are hard, small, round disks that were premade three days before served.

Wait a minute . . . I understand I am at a prison and I am just lucky to get a couple of hot meals each day. I hear you! I do! And yes,

I do say a prayer before eating every meal and thank Him for the good that I am about to partake in. Three . . . two . . . one . . . my stomach is making some funny noises! LOL!

Chapter 44

My New Friend

I t is one of those days when you look at yourself in the mirror and just want to cry. My job at work this morning was to sit with somebody who is currently on suicide watch and needs what LCI calls a suicide buddy. Being at a level 1 facility where inmates are serving short-term sentences, I didn't really think other inmates around me might be on a suicide watch. Everybody has a breaking point, so I shouldn't assume or judge others, not knowing their circumstances or background. My thought process as I was walking over to the G housing unit was I would sit there and stare at somebody for three to four hours and make sure he didn't harm himself. Well, I was mistaken. The morning went nothing like I thought, which was actually good news.

As I walked up the steps two at a time to the top range to room 223, I noticed a face pressed up against the small window, peering out curiously. I found out later that this gentleman's name was Christopher Barnes, and boy did he enjoy the company. He was originally from Atlanta, Georgia, and he was an avid Atlanta Braves baseball fan. Their number one fan, according to him. Since I am a huge Chicago Cubs fan, we already had something in common. You always need a topic to break the ice, and for us, it was baseball. Come to think of it—almost the whole time I sat there with Christopher, all we talked about was baseball. This was fine with me. Currently, with COVID-19 still rampant around the USA, there are no baseball games being played except the Korean Baseball League. I will be super polite when I say the Korean Baseball League does not interest me in the least.

The only other topic that Christopher—or as he said, "Call me Chris"—discussed was family. Baseball and family are my two favorite things to talk about with somebody. This might be the start of a great friendship. He mentioned that he just went through a divorce hearing with his wife. She was angry and frustrated with him, and she told him that she was done with him. She was not going to stick with Chris and try to get through this together. And get this—he used to be a teacher in the Fulton County Public School System in Georgia before his incarceration. He also has three kids, just like I do. God works in mysterious ways! I will never doubt this saying ever again. I did not share any information about myself with Chris yet. I was just a listening ear when he started to discuss his personal life. Next time, though, I will share with him about who I am and maybe even why I am here. When my replacement showed up, I felt good when I left Chris, heading back to the chapel for the rest of the day. Mainly, I thought that I just helped somebody like I used to on a daily basis.

Talking about helping someone, I turned on the television in the dayroom tonight, and what I saw caught my attention. There were many large protests in major cities in support of George Floyd, who was murdered by a policeman. Watching the footage of Mr. Floyd, who was saying he couldn't breathe, and the policeman not moving his knee from his neck was upsetting. Peaceful protests are always a good start, but obviously, more needs to be done immediately and for our next generation. The time is now to stop all this madness! Watching and experiencing the way some of the correctional officers treat us inmates has been eye-opening and agonizing. Most of the officers are ethical, just like the policemen on the street, but there are a couple who are just downright wretched.

I can think of a couple of acronyms that my cousin Leesa shared with me before my hearing that I have brought with me during my incarceration.

P: Pray   F: Forever
U: Until   R: Rely
S: Something   O: On
H: Happens   G: God

Whether it is George Floyd or somebody else involved in these traumatic events, we as a nation need to come together and be one—yes, the politicians and citizens. If we had more love in our hearts and are living spiritual lives, less shameful and pathetic episodes across the country would happen. This is what most US citizens believe, but still, to this day, we need a change. WE THE PEOPLE . . . how about listening to the song "Ebony and Ivory" over and over until we get the message? Just an idea.

I always wanted to be somebody who made a difference in people's lives when I was growing up. It definitely hurts somewhat to know that, as a principal, I was making a difference. I was such a positive person. Spending the day with Chris brought back those good feelings. Tomorrow morning, I am assigned to sit with Chris from 7:00 AM to 11:00 AM and keep him company. We have a lot to talk about besides baseball and our personal lives. I wonder if he knows that he is also helping me while we chat. I somewhat feel selfish for some odd reason because I am supposed to be there for him. Should I tell him that our chats help me too? Maybe that will help him knowing. It sounds like to me he just needs a friend. Well, he has one.

I talked with my dad and mom on the phone tonight, and I had a hard time composing myself discussing the children. Not thinking about your family and their struggles while you are incarcerated is virtually impossible. My mom reiterated to me how good a father I always have been, but sitting here writing this, it is hard to agree with her. Although I know she is right, my children need their father, and I am not at home with them for support. This conversation with my parents led to me calling the kids to see what they were up to at home. I shared with them a few things that happened to me in the last week. They enjoyed hearing about my new friend, Chris. MJ was excited to hear that he liked baseball, and Chloe was ecstatic when I told her he used to be a teacher. Both kids are curious and enjoy hearing about my time at LCI. I had a dream last night that I told them about before hanging up the phone, or should I say logging off my tablet. The dream was about me walking out of prison on my last day as a free man. I wonder how many times I will have that dream while I am here. So far . . . three.

Chapter 45

Your Voice Matters

I am writing while I am sitting here with Chris today. I thought it would be a good idea to write while we were discussing different things. We discussed so far lots of various topics, such as COVID-19, President Trump, George Floyd, protests, looting, professional sports, education, weather, and family. The time was flying by as it always does when I talk to Chris. He just lay down to take a nap, so I am taking this opportunity to write about something we talked about regarding education that caught my attention. Chris being a former teacher and me being a former principal—it was almost like having a staff meeting.

Both Chris and I think that the public school system needs to be dramatically reformed. The system currently in place has too much emphasis on testing and assessment. The teachers need more time to teach creative and innovative lessons that catch the students' attention. All of the technology available at the students' disposal gave them the opportunity to learn, discover, and explore. Depending on the school district, this is already happening in some states and cities to a certain degree. I would LOVE to be an educational consultant when I get my release from LCI, but it will NEVER happen. I am now a convicted felon, so my job possibilities will be extremely limited. This makes me extremely sad! I could go on and on . . .

Here is another thing that makes Chris and me perplexed— racial inequality and injustice. Two thumbs up to all the protestors for speaking out and peacefully protesting this month. C'mon, America, wake up! I am not going to sit here and preach about this topic since I have never lived in an African American man's shoes one day in my life. But when is enough, enough! This is 2020. Chris told me to write about this topic in my journal since we both agree. God bless you all!

Chris has not woken up from his nap yet. He said he had a rough night last night. I shared with him from 1 Peter 5:7 to cast all your anxiety on Him because he cares for you. It seemed like his ears perked up as we had a short conversation about Christ and letting him know he is not alone. Christ is always there for him to provide strength and eternal life by letting him in to help him.

Chapter 46

Say It Ain't So!

It has been one week since I last wrote in my journal, and all I ask is that you read the next paragraph and please understand that living at LCI or a similar intuition life is EXTREMELY difficult. There is so much time to just sit around and think about how unfair life really is at times. This week has been tough! No matter how bad your life is, there is always someone else struggling much worse than you. Much worse!

Dear Nyles,

I just wanted you to know that every time you came to sit with me, it was always my favorite part of the day. Your comforting words were exactly what I needed. Knowing how much pain I have caused, I am choosing to not extend my life any further. I am not sure if I am going to be successful with what I am planning on doing, but if I am, just know I consider you a friend. Your love for others is an inspiration, and you will be fine when you get out. Please realize you helped me, even though I decided to take my own life. I am at peace with my decision, and I did pray all day, asking Him for forgiveness about what I was going to do. It is a selfish way to end my life, but the pain I feel is too overwhelming. I also wrote a note to my family, apologizing to them and for all the pain I caused.

God bless,
Chris

I have been writing in my journal for almost a year, and this is the first time I don't know what to write. Life is short! You think you have problems? Could I have done more? I thought about calling the kids, but I knew I would cry during our conversation, so I didn't call. I prayed off and on for the past couple of days, and I knew what I needed to do. I NEED to get something off my chest, so I can move on today and every day forward. John 8:36 states, "If the Son sets you free, you will be free indeed." Here it goes . . .

Dear Jenny,

The hurt and pain I caused my best friend (you) is immeasurable. Hopefully, you will be able to move on with unsurmountable strength to do things that you didn't even think you were capable of. Please understand I am fully aware of the damage I left behind and will work daily in bettering myself to resemble the old Nyles that you once knew and loved. I have asked for Christ's forgiveness to get me through each day, and so far, he has granted this for me. And he will continue to do so. Reach out for him, too. He is waiting for you!

MJ, Chloe, and Jacob need both of us more than ever, and they are currently waiting on you for Direction. Your love and wisdom will be their light if they feel like they are in a dark place. May we both speak well of each other to our kids. Give them some Independence and freedom when they deserve it and let them grow as individuals. Keep the communication lines open, and they will come to us for advice. They will grow up so fast! Let them soar like eagles. I will miss you more than you will ever realize. I am so very thankful for our kids love and support. We have Amazing children!!

Love,
Nyles

Chris's sudden death hit me like a ton of bricks and puts things in perspective more than ever. Feeling sorry for myself is NOT an option. My three kids need their father, and the only way I can be there for them now is through my voice. My current situation is bleak, but my future is what I will make of it. I have battled an addiction like many others have and lost mightily. However, I will win in the end, and I know right now I have fixed myself and will NEVER be the old Nyles. My inspiration is my family and the unconditional love they have for me. If you are patient, you will hear from me again. God is good!

Made in the USA
Las Vegas, NV
12 September 2021